mafia betrayal

Syndicate of Sin

emilia rose

content warning

This book includes torture and references to child trafficking.

1

chiara

"FUCK, JUST LIKE THAT, BABY," Tommy, my boyfriend, said.

I stared at him, wide-eyed, through the crack between the door and the doorframe. A blonde bimbo bobbed her head on his cock, her eyes red and her cheeks stained with streaks of running mascara.

I yanked my purse higher up my arm, ready to grab the gun from it and shoot them both dead. Daddy had always shown me the right way to get rid of the people who had betrayed us.

But I couldn't kill Tommy yet.

I quietly walked out of his apartment and shut the door behind me. How much of an idiot was he? He was dating the daughter of the boss and thought it was a good idea to cheat. And, come on, if he was going to cheat, he could have at least found someone who could take his whole cock down her pretty little whore throat.

What a fucking idiot.

The phone in my bag buzzed. I expected his name to pop up with a sappy text, telling me that he would be home late tonight because Daddy was making him work late for the twelfth night in a row.

Daddy's name lit up my screen. I rolled my eyes, not wanting to deal with him after finding out what Tommy's late nights really were. But business came first for everyone in this family.

After speeding to Daddy's restaurant, Il Giardino del Cancio, in Lower Manhattan, I gave the valet the keys to my BMW. Two guards, dressed in sleek black suits and dark glasses, opened the doors for me.

Men with greasy hair and thick Italian accents entered and exited every day for business. Even the Feds who were paid off would visit for a drink and a chance to be with one of the family whores who had knockoff Chanel bags and fake tits.

I passed by the two women at the bar who were begging for attention from any man in the family. Cousin Tony would pick them both up later tonight. He had a thing for whores and could never stay faithful to his wife.

Nobody could stay faithful nowadays.

The men eyed me as I strutted to the back of the restaurant. I gave them a flirty smile. They all had a thing for me, but none of them had the balls to talk to me after what Tommy did to the last guy.

In the back, Daddy was eating a plate of penne. His gray trench coat was draped against the back of his chair. Two guards stood behind him.

When he saw me, he wiped his face with a napkin, stood, and wrapped me in a hug. "*Mio tesoro!*"

A man sat across from him, his fingers interlaced quite tightly on the table. His hair was lengthy but short on the sides and lightly curled on the top. And I could see a bit of dark tattoos underneath the cuffs on his button up.

"Sit, *tesoro*." Daddy pulled out a seat for me. "I want you to meet someone." He gazed over at the man who had a small scar under his left eye. "This is Alessandro."

We stared at each other. I couldn't be bothered to say much to him. Everything I was going to do to Tommy was racing through my mind.

"We have a shipment coming in the morning. I need you to be there when it's delivered to oversee that everything goes well," Daddy said.

I raised my brows. "Me?"

"This is what you wanted, isn't it?"

I nodded and sat up straighter. For three years, I'd been begging him to let me in on the business, but he had refused. He thought that it was a man's job. I wanted to ask why he had suddenly changed his mind, but I didn't dare open my mouth.

"Alessandro will be there with you. He usually does this kind of work."

Alessandro clenched his jaw as he looked at me with his hard gray eyes.

Daddy pushed his plate toward the center of the table and stood. "He will give you the details. Be there at three a.m." He gazed at Alessandro, who just nodded. "You're in good hands, *tesoro.*"

He leaned over to press a kiss on my forehead. "Don't make me regret this," he whispered in my ear.

I tensed and pressed my lips together.

Daddy picked up his jacket from the back of the seat and hung it over his shoulders. "I will let you two go over the plans."

When Daddy and his guards exited the restaurant, I exhaled. I would make sure that tonight went perfectly. No fuckups.

None of these mafia men thought a woman could keep up with them, but tonight was my chance to prove that I could. I didn't need a cheating boyfriend to take care of me anymore.

I had waited three years for this opportunity. The first step in my little plan was in place. Little by little, I was going to destroy Tommy, and today was day one. He had moved up in the ranks because of me, and I was planning to knock him six feet under.

Alessandro took out his wallet. "How much do you want?"

I furrowed my brow at him. "What're you talking about?"

"How much do I have to pay you to stay home tonight?" He flipped through tens of hundred-dollar bills.

I narrowed my eyes. "You think you can pay me off?"

He threw down all the bills from his wallet and put it back into his pocket.

"I'm not taking any money from you."

"Take it or leave it, *reginetta*."

"What's the address?" I asked, crossing my arms over my chest.

He paused for a long time, staring at me with a clenched jaw. "Why can't you be easy? Take the money and have *Tommy* do the work." Tommy's name rolled off of Alessandro's tongue with such distaste.

I nearly laughed. *I hate him too, stronzo. You're not the only one.*

"No," I said.

"You don't want to break a nail or, God forbid, get blood on one of your designer bags and fuck up this shipment, do you?" He raised his voice.

I placed my hands on the table and leaned closer to him. "Let's make one thing clear. If I break a nail or, *God forbid*, get blood on one of my designer bags, I'll just buy a new one. That's not a problem."

Alessandro pushed out his chair and stood abruptly. His gray eyes glared into mine. "I have one rule." He placed his palms on the table and towered over me. "Stay out of the fucking way tonight."

I raised a sharp eyebrow at him and stood. "Excuse me?"

"You heard me."

I followed him to the exit and snatched his elbow. "Speak to me like that again, and you won't even have a job, *stronzo*."

He grasped my chin in his rough hand. "Touch me like that again, and you won't like the consequences, *reginetta*."

"What's the address?" I asked through clenched teeth.

"3260 Flatbush Avenue. Brooklyn. Three in the morning."

<h1 style="text-align:center">2</h1>

chiara

TOMMY: **My place at 8pm, babe.**

Tommy: Just got to pick something up from Chiara's place. Be back soon 😍

I clenched my jaw, reading their stupid messages to each other. Since when did he ever use emojis? And the heart-eyes one, really?

Way to look desperate, stronzo.

When I had suspected that Tommy was cheating a week ago, I'd installed an app on his phone and hidden it among the iPhone's Productivity apps. He never looked there—obviously, since he hadn't deleted it by now. Desperate and stupid.

After sliding my phone into my purse, I picked up my bags of designer clothes from my shopping spree and walked into the building. My little talk with Alessandro had made me buy a whole new wardrobe, not because I didn't want to get my clothes bloody, but because I wanted to piss him off. The men in this family were getting really annoying, and they needed to be put in their goddamn places.

You'd best bet that I'd be doing that in a pair of red bottoms too.

From the garage level, I hit the button on the elevator and gazed at my phone, typing Alessandro's name into Google. By his thick Italian accent, I could tell that he hadn't been in New York for more than a few months. Daddy must've really thought he was good at what he did to fly him out from Italy and trust him with these shipments.

He couldn't even trust his daughter not to fuck up.

There had to be some dirt on him. All the mafia men were involved in scandals. It didn't matter if they were Italian, Irish, or Russian.

But when I searched his name, Google gave me no results. I sucked in my bottom lip. I had to get something.

The doors opened on the main floor for the lobby, allowing other residents on. Someone grabbed my phone from my hands and gazed at it.

"Who's this?" Tommy clenched his jaw, reading the name.

Great. I already have to deal with one stronzo later tonight, and now, I have to deal with Tommy being a dick.

"Someone who just started working for my dad." I reached for my phone, but he pulled it away.

"Why were you looking him up?"

"Good evening to you too," I said sarcastically before I could say something much worse and blow my cover.

"You're my girlfriend, Chiara." His words sounded so passionate, so protective, so loving, that if I didn't know differently, I would think he was just a jealous boyfriend, not a cheating one.

Men thought they could pull a fast one on you all the damn time, didn't they?

The doors opened, and I forced a stupid smile. "Don't be jealous, Tommy boy." I toyed with the ends of his hair behind his ear and stepped out of the elevator. "You know I have eyes for you and you only."

He pushed me into the wall, trying to be sexy. "You'd better," he said against my ear.

I turned to him and pulled him closer by the end of his tie. "Let me show you ..."

He smirked and pressed his lips onto mine. I pushed away the thought of his lips on her fake ones and tried to act like I wasn't planning his murder down to the very second. His hands roamed up my body, squeezing my breasts roughly.

After a few moments, he pulled away. His gaze lingered on my lips. "How about tomorrow?"

"You're going to make me wait?" Thank God. I didn't want to get any diseases from the *stronzo* and the whore.

"I have work tonight."

Work? Good excuse. Very creative. The stupid girlfriend definitely won't wonder why you've been working late every single night for the past twelve days.

I nodded, pretending to be that stupid girlfriend, and opened the door to my apartment. Tommy took my bags and brought them in for me.

After a few moments of lingering in the kitchen and searching through my stuff—*you know, acting like he cared*—he disappeared into the back room.

My phone buzzed, and a naked picture of the whore flashed onto the screen. She was in a tiny little black bra and even tinier panties. Everything about her was fake. F. A. K. E.

Tommy: I can't wait to get back an—

I wrinkled my nose and stopped reading his response. This was pathetic. How long was I going to have to endure this disrespect before I could put a bullet straight through his head?

A few moments later, Tommy reappeared from my bedroom with a briefcase. He planted a kiss on my lips. "Don't wait up for me. I don't know when I'll be home."

"Okay, hon." I gazed at him from the kitchen counter. "Be safe!" I really hoped he stayed safe tonight because he was my kill.

When the door closed, I reopened Google and searched Alessandro's name again. I needed something. Anything.

His online footprint nearly didn't exist.

The whole article was in Italian, and I wasn't fluent. I only knew the important words.

I pressed my lips together and hoped for the best as I hit the Translate button on the bottom of the screen. His name didn't appear until the end. He had been granted one whole sentence.

26-year-old Alessandro Russo from Sicily—allegedly connected with the Sicily Mafia—was released from prison after serving only thirteen months of his 56-month sentence for drug trafficking.

The article was over two years old, but that didn't matter. I had dirt on the man, and I intended to get more.

3

chiara

I ARRIVED EXACTLY twenty-five minutes early to the address, just to piss off Alessandro. He was going to regret ever ordering me to stay away from my family's business. Nobody had dared to talk to me like that, and I hated how easily he had done it.

Alessandro was rude, arrogant even. He probably thought that I'd be a useless mess, but I would prove him, Daddy, and all the other made men wrong. This would go as smoothly as the rest of Daddy's business deals.

Nobody was at the shipping docks yet, so I had time to run through the plan in my head again. I opened my purse and took out my baby—a 9mm—with my initials etched into the handle. Dad had given it to me for my fifteenth birthday.

The gun was loaded, all seventeen rounds ready to go in case anyone who wasn't involved with the business decided to show up. Daddy had said gangs would try to take some of the shipments when they were being moved.

After placing the gun back in my purse, I applied another coat of red lipstick and unbuttoned the top two buttons of my beige Misha Nonoo silk shirt. Whoever said a woman needed to dress conservatively to get the attention of a well-respected man obviously didn't know the power of red lips and a 9mm.

When two-fifty a.m. rolled around, the lot was still empty. I sighed, resting my head against the seat, and grasped the steering wheel. If Alessandro didn't show up, then I would do this by myself. I wouldn't fuck up like he expected me to.

Daddy was giving me one chance, and he already didn't believe in me.

3:00 a.m.

3:01 a.m.

3:14 a.m.

Empty.

I clenched my hand around the steering wheel. That *stronzo* had probably given me the wrong address so I wouldn't show up, making me look bad. Then, he could snitch on me to Daddy.

For the next three hours, I sped to every dock in all of New York City. My tires screeched around each corner. I messaged Alessandro. I messaged all of the guys I knew who would be at the dock this morning. I even thought about messaging Daddy, but I didn't want him to think I didn't have this under control.

Everyone seemed to want to fuck me over today.

The cobalt sky faded to powder blue over some of the buildings on the horizon. In less than an hour, rays of light would begin breaking their ways between the skyscrapers, and I had done nothing. Absolutely nothing.

I'd checked every single dock, except one.

West 79th Street.

Cars were leaving, one by one, through different exits. A cargo truck passed me as I sped into the lot. One of Daddy's men sat in the driver's seat. He had the damn audacity to wave at me.

I pressed down on the gas. Alessandro was going to regret this!

He was walking to his car with his phone pressed to his ear. I slammed on the brakes, nearly giving myself whiplash, and hopped out of my Benz.

"I will be by later," he said, gazing up at me. He clicked off the phone and slid it into his pocket. *"Reginetta."* A smirk stretched across his lips. "Finally decided to show up."

I pushed my hands into his chest. "You *stronzo!* I had to drive around all of New York because you'd told me the wrong address."

He chuckled. "I did no such thing."

"You will pay for this, Alessandro."

He took a threatening step toward me. "Is the princess going to tell her daddy on me?" He circled around me. "What're you going to tell him?"

I clenched my fists, wishing that I hadn't left my damn purse in the car. I would've already done more than hit him over the head with it.

He walked around me, stopping to stand behind me, dangerously close, and placed his lips by my ear. "You won't tell your daddy because you know he won't believe you."

My breath hitched. He wouldn't. And I'd bet Alessandro had volunteered to take me out so he could flat-out fuck me over like this. That had probably been his plan the whole time.

I poked my finger into his chest. "What's your damn problem?"

"You'd get in the way."

"You don't know that."

"Yes, I do." He stuffed his hands into his pockets and tilted his head. "Women like you—"

"Don't you dare finish that sentence! You know nothing about me." I seethed.

He clenched his jaw. "Daddy's little girl snags the perfect guy next door, gets everything she's ever wanted, doesn't have to work a day in her life … I know exactly who you are."

I crossed my arms over my chest. "You think I wanted this life?"

"I think you don't know any other kind. You wouldn't be able to survive without your daddy and all his money," he said.

He reached for the car door, but I snatched his wrist.

He wrapped his hands around my throat. "What did I tell you about touching me?" His thumbs pressed into the sides of my neck, making it hard to breathe. "What did I tell you, *reginetta*?" He slammed me up against his car. "Did I tell you not to?"

"What're you going to do about it?"

Those cold gray eyes glared down at me. He released a little pressure on my neck, his thumb trailing roughly down my jaw. I shoved him away, but he grinded his pelvis further into me and held me in place.

"You're a *stronzo*."

He shook his head and grazed his thumb over my lip. "*Ci provi troppo*." He pushed me away and opened his car door. "Don't fuck up the address next time, *reginetta*, and we won't have a problem."

Then, he shut the door on me and sped out of the lot.

4

chiara

THAT *STRONZO* WAS NOT GETTING AWAY with this so easily. I slammed the car door and started the car.

What was his problem? I would've done exactly what he needed me to, and he knew that. He knew I wouldn't pull anything because I needed to prove myself to Daddy.

So, why? Because he was another one of Daddy's men who thought so lowly of the women in this family that it was laughable.

I sped down the road, trailing after his car. Was I crazy for doing it? Maybe. But what was even crazier was, I saw Tommy's stupid car parked on the side of the road, next to a high-end breakfast restaurant, and I stopped.

Mr. Alessandro Russo would be dealt with later.

This was a more urgent matter. I'd seen him fucking the bitch before, but he never took her out. His bank statement had expensive purchases, which were for her and her only because I never saw that Mercedes or that $6K Cartier bracelet. But I knew for a fact that he never showed her off to anyone else.

Now, he was using my family's money to take her out on dates that he had not taken me on in weeks.

I pulled over to the side of the road, across the street from the restaurant, and waited for them. What had I ever seen in Tommy? He had to be one of the stupidest men on this goddamn planet.

Someone knocked on my window, making me jump. I gazed over to see a police officer staring at me through the glass. His brows were furrowed.

"Hello?" I asked politely.

"Hello. Are you Ms. Capitelli?"

I pressed my lips together. "Why?"

He chuckled. "Don't worry. I'm with Detective William."

"Detective William?"

"Yes."

I paused for a few moments, gazing back at the restaurant to see if Tommy had walked out yet. The door opened, and a tacky blonde walked out with her arm curled around Tommy's. Her head rested on his shoulder in an attempt to look cute.

"He wanted me to deliver a message to you," the officer said.

The woman on Tommy's arm had her breasts pushed up far beyond belief.

I mean, good for her, but does she have to look like that during breakfast? Jesus Christ.

Tommy wrapped an arm around her shoulders and drew her closer, a big smile on his face. He whispered something in her ear, and they shared a laugh.

"Ms. Capitelli?" the officer said.

Once Tommy and that bitch got into their car, I started mine.

The officer grabbed my hand on the steering wheel. "William needs to talk."

"Tell him that he can tell me himself." Tommy's car sped down the road. "I need to go now."

Without another word, I pulled onto the road. Tommy would drop her off, and then he'd drive to my place and tell me that he'd had a long night at work.

Instead of going right back home to hear his lame excuse, I drove to Il Giardino del Cancio. Daddy's guards urged me to wait outside since he had a very important guest inside. I walked in anyway.

I needed to make sure I talked to him before Alessandro had a chance to.

He sat across from a balding man and gave him the smile he always did right before closing a big deal. After they shook hands, Daddy lifted his gaze to meet mine. He clenched his jaw and dismissed the man.

Everyone left the room, including the guards. When the door closed behind his very important guest—a guest obviously more important than me—he turned to me, eyes ice cold.

"Chiara." He shook his head. "I gave you exactly what you wanted. I gave you a chance to run this family, and you blew it."

Alessandro had already told him, dammit.

"I was at the exact address he gave me, Daddy. He gave me the wrong place to meet—"

He slammed his fist down on the table. "Don't give me excuses, Chiara. I can see right through your lies."

"It's not an excuse!"

He grasped my arm, forcing me closer, and lowered his voice. "I gave you a chance. I wanted to see you run this family." *Lie.* "Do you know how bad it looks that you didn't show up? It looks like you aren't taking this job seriously, and I can't have you fucking this up for our family."

"Why don't you believe me? Is it because nobody wants a wom—"

He rolled his eyes. "Don't start with that shit, *tesoro*. You know I want to see you run this family."

"Then, why do you believe Alessandro and not me?"

"Alessandro has been in this business since he was seventeen. He knows exactly what he's doing. He knows exactly who he can trust and who he can't."

"So, are you saying that you don't trust me?"

He covered his face and groaned. *"Tesoro, tesoro, tesoro ..."*

"Is that why you gave Alessandro the address and not me?"

After a few moments of silence, he shook his head. "That's enough. If you are looking for another chance to redeem yourself, you need to take it up with Alessandro. You are dismissed."

My eyes widened. He was serious. Oh my God.

"But, Dad—"

"Go home, Chiara," he said. "Tommy is probably waiting for you."

Of course. How could I forget good-boy, suck-up Tommy?

"Don't forget the party tonight. I expect you to be there," Daddy said.

I pushed past him and rushed out the door.

"Good morning, *reginetta*." Alessandro walked into the restaurant, gazed back at me, and flashed me a smirk right as the door shut on my face.

I wanted to go back in and make him pay, but Daddy wouldn't believe me and wouldn't allow it. Killing Alessandro would just make more of a mess for Daddy.

But did it matter? He already didn't trust me—and he shouldn't.

5

chiara

"ALL THE MEN in this family are *stronzos*," Giorgia said over the phone. "What can you do?"

I clutched the pillow in my hand, wanting to rip it apart.

"So, will I see you at the party tonight?"

What a great friend. Giorgia had given me a one-liner and changed the subject so she didn't have to deal with it. If I hadn't needed to get it off of my chest, I would've shut my mouth, but Alice wasn't picking up the phone, and Giorgia was the only other *friend* I had left that I trusted.

"Giorgia." I shook my head. It wasn't even worth it. "Yeah, I'll be there."

The door to my apartment opened, and Tommy walked in with a big smile on his face.

"Hey, babe," he called.

I gave him a half-smile. *Fake it. Fake it. Fake it.*

"Is that Tommy?" Giorgia asked, suddenly interested in the conversation. "Tell him I said hi!"

I rolled my eyes and plastered a fake smile on my face. "Of course."

Everyone loved Tommy, it seemed. Everyone but me.

"Giorgia, I have to go. I'll see you tonight." I shut off the phone before she could respond to me.

Tommy pulled on his tie, loosening it. "Sleep well?"

After gathering all the patience I had left, I stood and helped him remove the damn tie. "Yes." I hung the tie off of one of the kitchen stools. "You're home late."

He ran a hand through his hair. The scent of strawberries lingered on his neck. He'd tried to hide it with an overwhelming heap of Axe cologne, but I still smelled it.

"Yeah." He nodded. "I had a big deal last night."

My fingers, quite tensely, unbuttoned the last few buttons on his shirt. "Nothing that you couldn't handle, I bet." I forced myself to kiss his cheek and then I gazed down at my feet. "I'm, uh, going to shower."

Before I slipped into the bathroom, Tommy peeked his head in.

"Your dad's having a party tonight. I bought you a dress." He opened the door wider and showed me a pretty royal-blue dress with a swooping neckline. Tommy sure did like his tits, huh? "We'll leave at six."

Daddy didn't have any more work for him tonight? I rolled my eyes. Goody-two-shoes Tommy had to keep up his image of the perfect guy to marry the boss's daughter and inherit the Capitelli millions, apparently.

His phone buzzed. Work calling again.

Once he left and shut my bedroom door, I frowned. I locked the bathroom door and started the water, letting the steam decorate the top of the mirror.

I stripped my clothes and put on the dress to see how it would fit. It was a few sizes too tight in the hip area and a size too loose in the bust. He'd probably gotten this dress for her. She would be able to fill it out perfectly, her boobs hanging out of it, basically screaming *fuck me* in it.

I tried to pull the bust tighter, tried pushing my breasts up, so the dress would look decent, so I would look decent. But it didn't work. This dress hadn't been made for someone like me. It had been designed for her.

What was wrong with me? Was I not enough for Tommy? Were my boobs not big enough? Was I not pretty enough? What did she have that I didn't?

A tear slid down my cheek. I gazed at myself in the mirror and wiped away the tear. I was stronger than this. Tommy wouldn't break me. The whore wouldn't break me.

Once I spent almost an hour in the shower, I walked to my bedroom to see Tommy sprawled out on my bed, drooling on my pillow.

Stronzo.

Since he was sleeping oh-so peacefully, I woke him up. If he was making me stay up all night, thinking about all of the things he was doing to her, then he wasn't going to get any sleep when he was here.

"Go take a shower. We need to leave soon."

He grumbled and dragged himself into the bathroom. I walked into my closet and shut the door. Obviously, the dress he had bought for *me* was not going to work for tonight, so I had to throw something together.

I wanted to wear something that screamed, *Look at me. Me. Me. Me. Me.*

Not her.

I picked out a wine-colored dress that accentuated my ass— because if you got it, you'd better be flaunting it. That was how Mom had lived.

Once I accessorized, I sat down on one of the couches in my walk-in closet and reopened Google. The article from yesterday about Alessandro was still up, so I decided to do a little more digging. I wanted something that I could use against him so he would have to give me another chance. He had secrets. Everyone in the family did.

The journalist's name was Greta Morelli. If she knew something —anything—it was worth trying to find her even if she didn't speak

English. Within moments, I found her email address and her work phone number.

The phone rang three times before someone answered.

"*Ciao. La Sicilia,*" a man said.

"Hello."

"*Un Americano. Un momento.*"

There was some fumbling on the line and then a woman spoke. "Hello. How may I help you?"

"Hello," I said. "May I speak to Greta Morelli?"

She was quiet for a few moments.

"You have the wrong paper," she said quickly.

"No, this is the—"

"Sorry, we cannot help you. Please don't call back."

The line went silent.

Dammit. I was going to have to get my information a different way.

"What're you wearing?" Tommy walked into the closet with a towel wrapped around his waist. "I bought you a dress for tonight."

I suppressed the urge to roll my eyes. "It doesn't fit." I stood up and did a twirl. "Don't you think this looks good on me?"

He paused for a few moments and walked over. "Are you wearing a push-up bra?"

"Yes."

"Oh." He looked disappointed, then pulled the top of my dress down a bit to see more of me. He shook his head. "Change. You'll look better in my dress."

We gazed at each other for a long time. Anything to please Tommy boy. He was the king, and I had to be his stupid little servant for a bit longer.

6

chiara

IN THE ELEVATOR, I pulled down the front of my dress, so it wouldn't look so loose and unflattering. Tommy stood behind me, gazing at me through the reflection. He eyed my breasts and snaked a hand up my body until he was roughly groping one.

"You're so sexy."

I tightened my grip on my purse.

When the elevator doors finally opened, I stepped away from him, trying to put enough space between us to calm down. If I didn't, I would surely ruin the plan.

Tommy grabbed my hand and pulled me to the restaurant that Daddy had reserved for the family gathering. The two guards at the door nodded at us as we walked in.

It wasn't even six-thirty p.m. yet, and half the family was already drunk. Men had Afterglow champagne glasses in their hands, women had tight bodycon dresses on, children of some of the members were already gossiping in the corner.

Daddy was sitting at a table with a few of the higher members. When he saw us, he nodded at us to come over. Tommy pulled me in his direction.

Thankfully, nobody—not even the men at the dock this morning—commented on my absence. Tommy didn't even seem like he knew, and I hoped it would stay that way. He was always the most vocal about providing for me, like I was incapable of doing it myself.

Someone wrapped their arms around me from behind.

Tommy turned around, jaw clenched, then relaxed. "Hey, Alice."

She gave him a small smile. Her hair sat in curls at her shoulders, and she had glittery purple eye makeup tonight.

"I need to talk to you," she said quickly, pulling me away from the men and Tommy.

Thank God. I couldn't get out of there fast enough.

When we were across the room, she arched a sharp brown brow. "What happened this morning? Everyone's talking about you."

My eyes widened. "Everyone?"

"Just Giorgia, but you know that means everyone."

Giorgia had to blab her big mouth. Now, everyone was really going to think that I hadn't shown up for work.

Alice gazed at me, giving me a once-over. "And what are you wearing?"

I clenched my jaw. "I'll tell you about it after a drink."

With one eye on Tommy and the other on all the liquor I could drown myself in, I pulled her to the bar.

Cousin Tony was already sitting at the bar with a drink in his hand, flirting aggressively with two family whores.

When he saw us, he held his hands up in the air. "Ahhh, Chiara and Alice!" He pulled us in closer to his beer belly and pressed a wet, disgusting kiss on our cheeks, his mustache rubbing against me.

The whores gazed our way, trying to accentuate their features to make themselves more attractive than us for Cousin Tony.

"How are my favorite cousins?"

"We're good, Tony," Alice said.

Tony nudged me. "How's Tommy?"

I forced a smile, which Alice definitely caught. "Tommy is great."

I gazed over at him. He was now talking to some of Daddy's guards near the door. Tommy could charm anyone with his smile and his talk. That was how he'd snagged me, and now, I was stuck with his ass.

Just then, the bitch herself walked through the door with another brunette. With her breasts pushed up and a fake fucking smile, she looked at Tommy, and I swore she winked at him.

My hands clenched under the bar so nobody would see them. Her dress was nearly identical to mine, except it was a burgundy color. It hugged her curves perfectly. She didn't have to pull the thing down to get it to fit; it just did.

The bartender pushed my drink across the bar, and I immediately threw it back.

Tommy watched as she walked to the bar on the opposite side of the room.

Way to keep it discreet, Tommy. Good going.

One of the guards said something that I couldn't quite make out, and they all began laughing. I pressed my red-painted lips together. Who even invited all these whores to the family parties? They were no-good gold diggers who wanted nothing more than a good time and everyone's money.

"Chiara," Alice said.

Cousin Tony had returned to his girls, his hands grazing over their bodies. I turned away from him, wanting to keep an eye on Tommy, but also not wanting to give anything away to Alice.

Alice cleared her throat and gazed at Tommy. "Does he need to be taken care of?"

"Now's not the right time, Alice."

"It's always the right time." She pursed her lips. "You know how I feel about it. I'm always up for it." She suggested the only thought getting me through each day.

Alice had never liked Tommy. She had warned me over and over not to get involved with him, but I hadn't listened.

"Alice, please. I don't want to talk about him right now."

She hopped onto the barstool next to me. "Well then, tell me what happened this morning. Because Giorgia acted like you got shot or something. You know how she blows things way out of proportion."

I nearly laughed. Thankfully, she wasn't here yet. I needed time alone with Alice. It had felt like forever since I'd last seen her.

"Daddy finally gave me the chance to oversee business this morning."

"Are you serious?" She smiled widely and pulled me into a hug. "*Amore!* That's great! I'm so happy for you."

After a few moments, I pulled away. "Not really."

She furrowed her brows. "Why?"

Someone leaned over the bar next to me. I pressed my lips together, immediately recognizing the tattoos on his forearms.

"Vodka," he said in that thick Italian accent.

Why had my days been going from bad to worse?

Alessandro had his baby-blue button-up rolled over his forearms. His gray eyes met mine, and he smirked. "*Reginetta,* it's good to see you again."

7

chiara

AFTER FLASHING ALICE A MILLION-DOLLAR SMILE, he held out his hand for her to shake like he was the politest guy in the whole damn world.

"Alessandro."

Alice blushed and shook his hand. "Alice."

I rolled my eyes and nearly smacked her hand away. "Leave us, *stronzo.*"

He brought his drink to his lips. "So very rude, *reginetta.*"

"Listen," I said, glancing back at Tommy, who was lingering by the whore's table, "I don't have time for your shit right now."

He smirked and slid onto the stool next to me. "It seems like you do. You sure did this morning, following me home and all."

"What is your problem?"

I literally didn't understand this man. He had told me the wrong address so he wouldn't have to deal with me, and now, he wouldn't leave me alone after I asked oh-so kindly. Bipolar much?

Alice gazed between us. "I'll leave you two."

"No."

"Nice meeting you, Alice."

Alice walked to her table, leaving me alone with the moron.

He hopped off his stool. "Well, I should be getting around. Too many pretty ladies here for Tony to keep all to himself."

See? Bipolar.

I snatched his arm. "No, you're not going anywhere. You're going to sit right there. You want to talk? We need to talk."

"Chiara."

I pulled my hand away from Alessandro's.

Tommy's arm wrapped around my waist from behind, gripping me tightly. "Who's this?"

Alessandro gazed between us for a moment more, and then I saw that stupid glint in his eye that told me he was about to screw me over. "*Reginetta*, you haven't told him about me?"

Tommy's fingers dug into my side. "*Reginetta?*"

I glared at Alessandro. "This is Alessandro."

Tommy eyed him for a few moments, probably trying to figure out if he could trust him or not. I guessed he chose not because he pulled me closer to his chest.

"Well, Alessandro, Chiara and I will be off."

He pulled me roughly off of the chair, his hand tightening around my upper arm.

This damn *stronzo*.

Alessandro smirked at me.

That damn *stronzo*.

"How do you know him?" Tommy sneered into my ear, still dragging me away from the bar.

"Daddy introduced me to him yesterday."

"And that's why he's calling you *reginetta?*" Tommy stopped and glared down at me. "You're lying."

My eyes widened. "No, I'm not!"

"How do you know him?" he asked again, jaw clenched.

I lowered my voice. "I told you, *stronzo!*"

"*Stronzo?* So, now, you're calling me names? Getting defensive over it?"

He grabbed my jaw roughly, but I pushed him away.

"Don't feel so special. He's a bigger *stronzo* than you are." I took a deep breath. *Don't blow your cover.* "Listen." I placed my hand softly on his cheek. "I'm sorry. He's just been getting on my nerves. He won't leave me alone."

Tommy clenched his jaw. "He's about to."

When Tommy stormed away from me and to the bar where Alessandro was flirting with Giorgia—who had walked in, like, half a second ago—I rolled my eyes.

Men. They had no sense sometimes. All you had to do was try to take what was theirs, and they flipped.

Tommy grabbed Alessandro by the collar and pressed him against the bar. Giorgia gasped loudly, nearly spilling her drink on herself. Don't ask me why I almost laughed.

Alessandro had a damn smirk on his face the whole time Tommy was threatening him.

After Alessandro said a few words, Tommy slammed him into the bar and stormed out of the room. I rolled my eyes. I wasn't going to go find him. Fuck that guy. He could cool off with the whore in the restroom and get caught by Daddy for all I cared.

Alessandro gazed over at me and winked, then turned back to Giorgia.

I walked to Alice's table and collapsed next to her, resting my head on her shoulder. "I need a girls' trip away from all this shit."

"You mean Tommy?"

"Yes."

She smiled at me and stared back over at Alessandro. "Okay, so are you going to tell me who that is and why you seem to be so damn close with him? What am I missing? I've never seen him at any family parties before."

"Don't ask me. I have no idea why he's here, but I wish I had never met him," I said.

"Oh, come on." She pushed my shoulder. "You don't wish someone like him—look at him"—she glanced over at him and sighed deeply—"would sweep you off your feet and take you away from Tommy boy?"

"I don't care how attractive he is. He's an asshole. Daddy gave me one shot last night, and Alessandro screwed it up for me."

I explained everything that had happened since the last time I had seen her, which was over two weeks ago. From Tommy to Alessandro to the whore.

Unlike Giorgia, Alice knew about the way Tommy really treated me. She knew how screwed up he was, and now, she knew that he was a big fat cheater. I looked across the room as the whore walked in, displaying her chest to whoever wanted to see it.

"She's over there."

Alice, again, raised a brow and grabbed her purse. "You want me to take care of her? Because I got my gun in my purse, loaded and ready for a good time."

I nearly laughed and pulled her purse away from her. "I don't need Tommy to be suspicious. I'm working on revenge."

She relaxed a little. "So, you're going to let him get away with it?"

I smirked. "For now."

After a few moments, Tommy walked back into the room, looking *oddly* calmer than when he had stormed out. Instead of walking back to me, he sat with Daddy and talked to him a bit. He and Alessandro were both at his table, talking about something I didn't care about.

All I needed was for them not to kill each other. They could fight all they wanted, but no bullets in the head or the heart. I needed Tommy alive to get my sweet revenge and Alessandro alive to get another chance at the business.

As the night wound down, I found myself outside on the patio with my only friend at the moment—a glass of Afterglow champagne. Alice had had some of her own business to do, so she had left me alone with Giorgia. Then, Giorgia had ended up leaving with Cousin Tony. Not my first choice in a guy, but she had to do whatever she had to do.

I glanced at the whore through the glass door. Tommy had

approached her table and started chatting *innocently* with her and her friend. He had no damn respect. None. Absolutely none.

"*Reginetta*," Alessandro said, way too close. He placed a forearm on the railing next to me.

"Why can't you leave me alone?"

"I'm just admiring your beautiful city."

He leaned over the railing, gazing at Lower Manhattan. I had the urge to push him off the edge. *Admiring the city, my ass.*

"Your daddy told you that you couldn't work anymore? That's a shame. You shouldn't have let him down."

"You shouldn't have been let out of prison," I said.

He clenched his jaw.

"Oh, did I hit a nerve? My apologies." I gave him the fakest smile I could muster.

"How do you know about that?"

I shrugged my shoulders, staring at his clenched jaw. "I know a lot about you."

He stared at me for a few moments, then laughed. "You know nothing about me." He tilted his head and stepped closer to me. He glared at me with those dangerous eyes. "But you're right; I shouldn't have ever left prison. That way, I wouldn't have ever met you, *reginetta*. Out of all the *whores* here, you're the saddest one to deal with."

And before I could stop myself, I threw the glass of champagne in his face.

8

chiara

LIQUOR DAMPENED the perfect locks on his head and dripped down from the stray pieces of hair onto his shirt, soaking it right through. I arched a brow at the wet rat in front of me. He deserved nothing less. If he didn't know when or how to leave me alone, then I would teach him.

That sinister look crossed his face again. His eyes darkened, and he clenched his jaw. He took the half-full glass in his hand and poured it right over my head before I could step out of the way.

I let out a scream and pushed my hands into his chest, shoving him back. "What is your problem?!"

I pushed him again and again, all the way to the side of the balcony, and he let me. I stepped closer to him until he was nearly pressing into it. He had that stupid smirk on his face, so I pushed him again.

"Damn you!"

"Stop pushing me."

I pushed him again.

He snatched my wrists in one of his hands and grabbed my chin with the other. "And this is exactly why I didn't want you to come last night. You don't listen."

"No, you didn't want me to come last night because the oh-so-great Alessandro wanted to screw me over."

He twirled us around and pushed me into the side of the balcony, holding me in place. "And why would I want to screw you over? What do I have against you?"

"I don't know yet." I poked a finger into his chest. "But I'm going to find out what happened in Italy, and when I do, I will screw you and Tommy and Daddy into the next fucking century."

God, everyone in this family just kept getting on my nerves. Why couldn't I be left alone? Why couldn't I oversee business, and that was it?! I'd stay out of everyone's fucking hair, but every one of these men wanted to fuck me over in some way, and I didn't even know the reasons why.

"Let me oversee the next shipment, and I won't look any deeper into you," I said.

He arched a brow and scoffed. "You're trying to threaten me now?" He smirked. "You know, it's kind of cute, *reginetta*. Like a little child throwing a tantrum when they don't get their way."

"I'm not the one acting like a child."

He stepped closer to me, leaning his head down, chuckling low. "Look any further into me, and I promise I'll shoot a bullet straight through this pretty little head of yours." He tapped my temple. "I don't care who your daddy is. I will kill him, too, if I have to."

I tried pushing him back with one of my hands, but he held me in place and tilted his head.

"So, *reginetta*, what do you have against Tommy?" His voice was somehow more playful than it had been a moment ago.

"What're you talking about?"

"I can see why you're angry with me and with your daddy, but Tommy—the golden boy?" He moved beside me, still holding my chin in his hand, and made us gaze through the window.

Tommy was talking to the whore and her friend, along with another one of Daddy's men.

Alessandro placed his lips next to my ear. "What do you have against him?"

He was prying for information to destroy one of us, like I was prying for information to destroy him. But he wasn't going to get anything out of me.

"That's not your problem." This time, I really pushed him away and stormed to the door.

"*Reginetta.*"

I stopped by the glass door. Daddy and most of the men weren't here anymore. But the guards who were here still sat at the whore's table. They were all laughing with each other, having a good time, pouring more Afterglow wine and champagne.

Damn Tommy, the dumbass. He wrapped an arm around the back of her chair *innocently*, but didn't particularly get close to her, unlike Cousin Tony did with his women.

"*Reginetta.*"

Liquor dripped from my hair onto my dress—or maybe that was rain. I pulled the door open.

Fuck Tommy.

I marched right over to him.

He gazed up at me. "Why're you all wet?"

"It's raining. I would like to go now."

One of the guards leaned over and whispered something in Tommy's ear.

He nodded and stood. "I have to go. Work calls. Will you get home safe?"

Sure, I'll get home safe.

He pressed his lips to mine and walked out with the guard. I smiled *sweetly* at the whore, who smirked up at me. She stood with her friend.

"It's getting pretty late. We should get going." She extended her hand to me. "It was nice to meet you."

I smiled tightly. *Nice to meet the woman I'm going to fucking kill later.*

9

chiara

I WALKED out of the restaurant, my hair basically matted to my head, my dress soaked all the way through. I needed a damn shower after Alessandro and his little stunt. Sure, I was the one who had started it, but he hadn't had to be the one to end it. That was my job.

My phone buzzed with a text from an unknown number.

Unknown: 5th Ave and 40th. 1:30.

I checked the clock, gazing at the bright white numbers that read *11:21 p.m.* I had enough time to shower and drive there without Tommy noticing. Since he was out on actual business tonight, I was hoping that he would be gone all night long.

The elevator doors began closing ahead of me.

I jogged to it. "Hold the elevator!"

Before it could close completely, I snuck my hand through, and the doors reopened. I stepped in, saw Alessandro, and immediately wanted to walk back out.

I pulled my purse higher up my shoulder and waited for the elevator to open on the ground level. Alessandro followed me out. Conveniently, he had parked right across from me.

"Good night, *reginet*—"

"Fuck you, *stronzo*."

He suddenly stopped and grabbed my hand.

I yanked my hand away from his. "What do you think you—"

Three gunshots rang out through the night. He ducked behind my car, pulling me with him.

"Fuck." He shook his head and pulled a gun from the waistband of his pants. "Stay here."

He looked through the car windows for a moment, then stood. He pointed the gun toward his car and pulled the trigger, then pulled it twice more in different directions. A window shattered, its glass falling onto the ground.

I gazed under the car, seeing feet walking toward us from the left. Alessandro walked out from behind the car. My heart thumped against my chest. I had only been in a shoot-out once before. The night Mom had died.

And no matter how much I hated Alessandro, I couldn't let him die like Mom had.

I unzipped my purse and grabbed my gun. Besides, no way I was going to let him have all the glory and treat me like I could do nothing.

From beneath the car, I aimed my gun at the man's kneecap and shot, making him collapse to the ground. I hopped up and watched Alessandro walk to the man, press his shoe into the man's hand, and shoot him straight in the head.

Alessandro looked back at me, jaw clenched. "I told you to stay there."

I crossed my arms over my chest and walked over to him. "I saved your ass. A simple *thank you* would do."

Alessandro put the gun back into the waistband of his pants.

"Who is he?" I asked, bending down to pull the man's wallet or phone out of his pocket.

Alessandro grabbed my arm and pulled me quite harshly away from the man. "Nobody you need to worry about."

"Well, he shot at us, so, yes, I think I need to worry about him."

He shook his head, his face becoming paler. "Leave it alone. It's too risky for you. I told you, you'll just fuck things up for me." He dragged me to my car and opened the door. "Get in."

The light from inside the car flooded out. His baby-blue shirt was stained red with blood near his hip bone. He covered it with his arm, hiding it from me.

I knotted my brows. "You're shot."

"No shit. Now, get in the car and leave."

He continued to stand by the car, one hand on the top of the door, the other clenched like he was trying hard not to show any emotion.

Men. Always had to be so prideful. It would kill them one day. Natural selection at its finest.

I could leave him in the parking lot, bleeding out, but I needed him alive. He was going to give me a second chance, whether I had to force him to or not.

"I can help you," I said, gazing at the wound.

"I don't need your help."

"I know someone who can take the bullet out."

"I can take it out myself."

I clenched my jaw and dug my finger into his side, close to his wound. "Get in the damn car, Alessandro."

He winced as my finger dug into him deeper, threatening to hurt him. "You're fucking crazy."

I pushed him to the passenger side, then slammed the door in his face. I hopped into the car and sped out of the lot, dialing Ray's number.

"Meet me at my place now. Bring something to remove a bullet."

"Chiara, are you ok—"

"Just do it."

I ended the call and focused on finding the quickest route back to my apartment. As I took a turn onto Fifth, a car sped out of a side street and began tailing me. He drove closer and closer, his high beams shining brightly into my car.

"*Qual è il loro fottuto problema*?" Alessandro shook his head and removed his gun from his waistband again. "Step on it."

I pressed my foot to the floor, and we sped down Fifth Avenue, running red lights and skirting around bends. Someone began to shoot at us. The back windshield broke, the glass littering the floor.

"*Vai! Vai!*" Alessandro shouted, pointing ahead, like I already wasn't hitting one hundred miles per hour.

"Will you please tell me who the hell these guys are?"

Alessandro reloaded his gun, opened the window, and stuck one hand out of the car. "Sicilian Mafia. Is *reginetta* happy now?"

He shot twice, and the car swerved.

"Fuck me. This is not how I wanted tonight to go."

"Then, drive!"

I stepped on the gas, pressing it down as far as it would go. I couldn't lose them, no matter how many turns I took or how fast this car drove. They were on my ass, and they weren't leaving.

There was one way I knew I would be able to get rid of them. I slammed on the brakes, made a quick U-turn around a bend, and drove as fast as I could to the dock that Alessandro had made me wait at yesterday.

I continued to speed as Alessandro shot at the men behind us. The car swerved into a building, the airbags blowing up. I sighed in relief, stupidly thinking that we had lost them, when another car pulled up behind me.

Alessandro swore under his breath and pulled himself back into the car, reloading his gun. "I hope you know where you're going."

I had the urge to say something rude to him, but I shut my mouth and focused on getting to the dock.

When we finally approached it, I pulled off the side of the road, steering straight for the water.

The car behind us followed, and I called to Alessandro, "Shoot out his left tire when I tell you to."

"What?"

I pushed down on the gas. "Just do it! Now!"

He shot all seventeen bullets into the front tire of the car behind us as we approached the edge of the dock. I slammed on my brakes, and their car pulled to the left at full speed and drove right into the water.

My heart raced as I put the car in reverse and backed out onto the road. Alessandro rolled his window up and leaned against the seat, clutching his stomach.

Then, I drove to my apartment with a broken back windshield and bullet holes covering my car.

10

chiara

I SWERVED into my parking spot and hopped out of the car, examining the damage. My baby Benz was absolutely ruined. Holes in the car, the glass blown out, and blood soaking into the front seat.

Tommy couldn't see this. I had to keep it away from him at all costs.

After eyeing one of my neighbor's many covered cars, I pulled the cover off of it and threw it over my car. I would buy him a new one. He had all the money in the world. I doubted that he would mind anyway.

Alessandro clutched his stomach and leaned against the car. We walked into the elevators, and I hit the button for my floor. He leaned against the side of the elevator and closed his eyes, trying to take even breaths.

"Would you like to tell me why the Sicilian Mafia is after you? I thought you were one of them."

He clenched his jaw. "I told you to stay out of my business."

I placed my hand on my hip and turned away. "Fine."

When the elevator doors opened, I pulled Alessandro down the hallway to my apartment. The doctor stood in the hall, waiting for me. He widened his eyes, gazing down at Alessandro's wound.

It was bleeding much more profusely now, drenching his shirt and hand.

We rushed into the apartment. I told Alessandro to sit on one of the kitchen stools, thinking that it would ruin the least amount of furniture.

The doctor set his tools on the table.

"Take off your shirt," I said.

Alessandro gazed up at me. "Why don't you remove it? I kind of have my hands full, *reginetta*."

I rolled my eyes and undid the buttons on his shirt, peeling it off of him. My eyes flickered to his sculpted chest.

His eyes darkened. "You can check me out all you want when I'm not bleeding to death."

The doctor pulled out some sort of tweezers and told Alessandro to relax. Before he could remove anything, I placed a hand on his shoulder.

Alessandro shook his head up at me. "What are you waiting for?"

"You're going to give me another chance."

"No, I'm not."

I stepped closer to him, jaw clenched. "It wasn't a request. It was an order."

"And who are you to order me around?"

"The woman who could either save your ass right now or let you bleed out so damn slowly that you'd wish I'd put a bullet straight through your head."

He tensed as I pushed my thumb against his wound. "One fucking chance."

I stepped back, wiped my thumb onto my dress, and watched the doctor thrust his tweezers into Alessandro. His chest muscles tightened. I looked down at them, noticing a bullet scar on his left shoulder and another near his ribs.

He gazed at me, no hint of a smile. "It doesn't get easier,

reginetta. Each bullet hurts like a *puttana,* in case you were wondering."

I mustered up a fake smile. "I wasn't." I crossed my arms over my chest. "Now, tell me why the Sicilian Mafia is after you."

The doctor removed the bullet, pulling it out with his tweezers. He gave me a towel and told me to hold it over his wound. I pressed the towel—a little too hard—against his stomach. He winced. *Good.*

"Was, *reginetta.* I was one of them." He sat back, smirking. "Wanted to take a break and relax in America."

"Your life won't get any easier here."

"Because you keep getting in the fucking way."

I pressed into his wound, making him wince again. "What're you running from?"

"I don't run."

"So, what, you're a snitch? Is that how you got out of jail earlier than you should've?"

He shook his head and clenched his jaw. "I'm not telling you any more."

I pulled the gun out of my purse. I had him where I needed him. Holding the gun up to his temple, I smirked. "You *will* tell me everything I need to know."

11

chiara

"WHAT? Are you going to shoot me?" He scoffed and gazed right up at me, that stupid-ass smirk stretching across his lips.

Ray froze, letting Alessandro bleed out. Good. I'd taught him well.

I tilted my head, staring down at those eyes that I hated almost more than Tommy, but I couldn't hate anyone more than that *stronzo*.

I cocked the gun back a bit. "Eventually."

"I don't believe it."

"Let me show you then." I pressed the tip of the gun right into his wound, making sure to get it really deep in there. My finger hovered over the trigger as I turned the gun sideways.

He winced again and clenched his jaw. "Fuck you, *reginetta*."

"Three …" I pressed it deeper. "Two …" Deeper.

He began ranting in Italian, his full pink lips moving so fast that I couldn't catch a word he was saying.

"Now, Alessandro."

Someone knocked on the door. I pushed out a breath, not willing to give up my position over him. This was my chance to get every-thing I needed from him. Nobody was going to ruin this moment for me.

The knock turned into a forceful bang.

"Police! Open up!"

Alessandro narrowed his eyes at me. "Police? Why do you have police at your apartment?"

I sighed in annoyance and threw the gun onto the table. "Maybe they're here to take your ass back to jail," I uttered under my breath.

He banged again, and I rolled my eyes.

Was it one-thirty a.m. already?

Alessandro stood up abruptly, making Ray throw his hands up and shake his head in annoyance. Blood spewed from his wound. "What are you doing?"

"I'm going to answer the door."

"Without checking?"

"It's the police."

He shook his head. "You can't just go ahead and open the door for anyone." He grabbed my arm and held me back. "Don't be that stupid, *reginetta*."

I arched a brow and pulled my arm out of his grip. "I'm not being stupid. I'm waiting for him."

He lowered his voice as we walked closer to the door. "For a cop?"

"Yes, for a cop."

The officer knocked again, this time more forceful. I grumbled and opened the door.

William and the man I had seen earlier were standing outside the door, their hands on their guns. When they saw me, the worried expressions dropped from their faces. William's gaze traveled between me and Alessandro, then fixed on his bullet wound.

"What happened here?" Detective William asked.

I gazed outside the door, making sure nobody was watching, and then I ushered them in. "What are you doing here? We had a meeting spot."

He placed his hands on his hips. "We did, but it's past our meeting time, your car has bullet holes in it, and there is blood in the elevator and on your door. I thought something had happened to you."

I playfully rolled my eyes. "Oh, does someone care about me?"

"Don't feel so special." He smirked and rocked back on his heels. "I care about your safety for a reason. It's my job." He gazed over at Alessandro, who was staring at us with his brows furrowed.

I nodded to my bedroom, and he walked over with me.

"What do you need?" I asked.

He pushed me against my door and pushed his lips to mine. "You."

My eyes widened slightly, but I went with it. I hadn't seen him in over a week. He kicked the door closed with his foot and immediately pulled my dress straps down, waiting for nothing and taking what he thought was his. He left small kisses down my neck until he reached the middle of my chest. Then, he paused. "Why does your skin smell like alcohol? And why are you all … sticky?"

I took a deep breath and pulled the straps back up. "Way to make a girl feel sexy," I said, playfully pushing him away.

Now was not a good time for this. Alessandro would probably walk right into the room while William was in the middle of fucking me senseless. Who knew what he would end up thinking if we even stayed in my bedroom too long together? He'd probably tell Daddy I was fucking a cop on my off time, behind cheater Tommy's back.

William sat on the bed with me, and I drew a finger down his neck.

"What do you really want to talk about?"

"I have information on your mother's case."

My eyes widened. "You do?"

He nodded.

"Well, what? What is it? Did you find the man who killed her?"

He unlocked his phone and gave it to me. There was a file open on it. I read through its contents, my eyes growing wide.

"You're fucking with me."

He grimaced.

"This can't be real. It can't."

When he didn't say anything, I stood and shook my head.

Someone from the Capitelli family had ordered a hit on my mother.

12

chiara

I GAZED down at the phone again and ran a hand through my hair. "Is this all you have?"

"We're working on it," he said, taking his phone from me.

My heart tightened. I needed to tell Daddy that there had been a hit on her and that it had come from this family. It wasn't a neighboring gang or family that didn't like us or wanted revenge. This had been from someone close to us.

"What about Tommy?"

He shook his head. "Nothing yet."

I stepped toward him. "Am I paying you 100K for you to sit on your ass?" I looped my finger in his belt loop and pulled him closer, drawing another finger down his gun. "Because sitting on your ass all day is not what I'm interested in. I'm interested in information about my mother's death *and* my boyfriend."

"And information is what you'll get."

"I'd better." I trailed my finger down the zipper of his pants, feeling his hardness.

Oh, how fun it was to toy with him. Men thought with the wrong head sometimes—make that *all the time.*

"God, I love when you do that."

I pressed my red-stained lips to his. One lingering kiss. He placed his hands on my hips, drawing me closer, but I pulled away.

"Get me information, and I'll give you more."

He shook his head and rocked back on his heels, like the cop I had known for years. I gazed at the small wrinkles by his eyes. If I wasn't *dating* Tommy and he wasn't a police officer, I would truly consider dating William or allow myself to actually feel something for him, but I couldn't.

He was strictly for my own personal use.

I fixed myself in the mirror and kissed him once more on his lips, making sure he wouldn't forget what he would get if he got me all the information I needed.

When we walked out of the room, I made sure to keep my distance from him. Alessandro was watching our every move, never moving his hand from his gun. I gave Alessandro my best scowl and walked William and his partner to the door.

"I will be in touch as soon as I can," he said quietly.

When they left, Alessandro was leaning against the counter with his arms crossed over his bare chest. A large bandage was covering his bullet wound. Ray placed a bottle of painkillers on the counter next to him.

"Thank you, Ray," I said.

"I do it for the money." Then, he left too, leaving Alessandro and me.

"Strike a deal with the department?"

I clenched my jaw. "No, and it's not any of your business what I do with him."

"Well, as you said before, we are working together now, so if you're fucking a cop, you're putting us both in danger."

I rolled my eyes. Like he actually cared about being in danger. We had almost died because the Sicilian Mafia had put a hit on him. And he was scared about a couple of cops.

"And what about Tommy?" His biceps flexed.

"Do you just assume things? I'm not sleeping with the cop."

"Whatever you say, *reginetta*." He pushed himself off of the counter and walked around the apartment, then looked at me like he was waiting for something. "Are you going to get me a shirt that's not covered in blood, or do you want to continue to check me out?"

"You wish," I said as I walked down the hallway to retrieve a shirt from Tommy's closet. It was one I had gotten him for our six-month anniversary—when I still thought he loved me. It was a stupid shirt that he had stuffed in the back of his closet and never wore, not even for lounging around. So, he wouldn't notice if it was taken.

"It has a cartoon on it," Alessandro said.

"Well, it's that, or you walk home naked."

He put on the shirt. "Not even going to ask me to stay the night, *reginetta*?" The sleeves were fitted tightly around his biceps, but he looked damn better than Tommy ever would in it.

I pointed a finger at him. "I don't need you getting any ideas."

"Well"—he smirked—"it's a bit too late for that one, don't you think?"

I rolled my eyes and grasped the door handle. "Where and when am I meeting you for business?"

He leaned a shoulder against the doorframe. "At your father's restaurant. Tomorrow. Ten."

"A.M.? P.M.?"

He cracked a smile. "P.M. And keep Tommy at home."

13

chiara

AFTER WASHING DOWN THE TABLE, stools, and floor—making sure no more of Alessandro's blood was left in the kitchen—I threw all of the bloody paper towels in the garbage, along with his shirt.

Then, I did the only other logical thing there was to do when you were trying to hide your car, which had hundreds of bullet holes in it and a shattered back windshield, from your cheating boyfriend so he wouldn't get angry and ask questions. I removed the plates and drove it to the farthest junkyard I could find.

Not only did I want to avoid Tommy finding out what had happened, but I also wanted to avoid the Sicilian Mafia. I didn't know what kind of people they had in the States already. They were Alessandro's problem, and he would have to deal with them himself.

So, without leaving a smidgen of evidence behind to link the car to me, I called a cab to bring me all the way back home.

Before I went upstairs, I checked the garage. Tommy's car was parked next to my empty spot. I rolled my eyes, trying to come up with a good excuse as to where I had been because he was going to ask or assume.

When I walked into the apartment, Tommy was leaning against the counter with his arms crossed over his chest and his jaw clenched.

"You're home late." He stalked toward me.

Great. Here we go.

"How was your night?"

I closed the door behind me. "Good."

"I bet it was." His voice was gruff and terribly chilling. "Where were you?"

"Alice needed me to help her get out of a situation with this guy at a bar."

He chuckled, but there was no lightness in his voice. "Alice." He said her name like he didn't believe me. "Do you mean Alessandro?"

"No." I pressed my lips together and hiked my purse up my shoulder.

"You left the party with him."

He took another threatening step toward me, trying to intimidate me, but I placed my hands on my hips.

"No, I didn't."

"Don't give me that bullshit, Chiara." He raised his voice.

"It's not bullshit." I shook my head. "You weren't even there. How do you know when I left or with who? Stop making assumptions about me."

"Someone saw you leave with him."

"Who?"

"Karrie." He said her name like he had never spoken it before, like it was so new and unfamiliar to him, like he wasn't fucking her behind my back.

I clenched my jaw. So, that was the whore's name. *Karrie.*

That bitch had probably waited until I left to follow us out. She was watching me. She obviously knew who I was. She didn't know that I was going to be the one to kill her and her precious Tommy.

I didn't care that her fucking name was Karrie. I cared that he had the audacity to bring her name up in our conversation. So, I was going to put him on the spot—hard.

"Who's Karrie?"

He didn't react like I wanted him to, but he reacted exactly how I'd expected.

"Don't try to get out of this."

He was the one trying to get out of this. He was the one who had brought her name up.

"He was here." His breath smelled like hard liquor.

He was probably this moody because he hadn't gotten a chance to fuck the whore tonight.

"No, he wasn't."

I stepped closer to him and brushed my hand against his jaw, the way he loved. "Why would I be with him? He's been nothing but rude to me. He's a disgusting *stronzo* that I have no use for."

"No use?" he asked.

That was all he had gotten out of that.

He smacked my hand off his face and grabbed it, tugging me closer. "I'm tired of your lies. So fucking tired of them. You're mine. How could you even think about cheating on me with him?"

"Tommy," I said, forcing myself to keep my cool, "I'm not cheating on you. I promise."

He spun me around and bent me over the counter. He snatched my neck. "I'm going to show you why you are mine."

Before I could stop him, he pulled down my pants and his. He thrust himself into me—bare.

I had to keep this act up a little longer—just a little longer. He didn't feel good inside of me—hadn't for months. But it would all be worth it. It would.

He grabbed on to my hips, thrusting himself inside of me, harsh —terribly harsh. He pushed my face down onto the kitchen counter.

"Harder," I said.

He thrust harder into me, not stopping until he came inside of me. He pulled out, letting his cum drip down my thighs, and walked out of the room and to the bathroom. I followed him and hopped into the shower with him.

He pushed a hand through his wet hair and sighed. "I've had a rough night."

I wrapped my arms around him. He gently grabbed my face.

"You know I love you, right?" He smiled. "That I would do anything for you, even kill that fucking asshole?"

I grabbed on to his hand, stroking it slowly. "It's okay," I said, referring to what had just happened.

But it wasn't okay. I was counting down the damn minutes until I could kill him.

"I love you more than anything."

"I love you too, Tommy. I love you too."

14

chiara

DADDY GAZED at me from the middle of the room, brows furrowed. "What're you doing here this late, *mio tesoro*?" He sat next to me on one of the barstools and gently shook the glass in his hand.

There were only a few stragglers in his restaurant this late at night. Thankfully, none of them were any of the whores. Some of the men smiled at me behind Daddy's back, and I had no shame in giving them *the eyes* and flirting back with them.

After presenting me with the most beautiful platter of cheese and crackers and filling up Daddy's glass, the bartender was dismissed.

"Waiting for Alessandro."

It was 9:58 p.m., and that damn man still hadn't shown his face. If this was another trick, I was going to do far worse than draw a fucking gun on him.

"Alessandro, huh?" He shook his head and sipped his drink. "You won't find him here. He's on business tonight."

"Actually, I'm going—"

He nudged me. "Why don't you spend the night with Tommy?"

Sure, Daddy. I'll spend the night with Tommy and his whore. Sounds great.

I stopped myself from rolling my eyes. Another way he was trying to steer me away from this business. But I couldn't see the problem with me taking on more of a leadership role. We were family by blood from the womb, not blood from a fucking gun. He should trust me more than some of the other family members.

The door opened, and Alessandro walked in.

Daddy smiled, like Alessandro was the best thing to ever happen to him, and slapped a hand on his shoulder, squeezing a little too tightly. "What are you doing here?"

"I'm going on business with him," I said.

Alessandro nodded. Daddy sucked in a breath.

"*Mio tesoro.* Oh, I don't think that's a good idea."

Here we go again.

"Tonight is a big deal. It's not like the last time, which you missed."

I glared at Alessandro. *Missed.*

When I turned my attention back to Daddy, I forced my best smile. "Well, Alessandro kindly offered to take me. I won't disappoint you this time."

Daddy looked back at Alessandro, his jaw clenched slightly but enough for me to catch it. "Alessandro," he said, "a word."

They walked to the opposite side of the restaurant. Alessandro gazed over at me, a smirk teasing the right corner of his lip. Daddy looked over, and I turned around, *not* wanting to eavesdrop.

"*Abbiamo un accordo,*" Daddy said quietly. He could never speak quietly. I used to hate that when I was a kid and he was scolding me in front of everyone, but now, it was very beneficial.

Accordo. I might not be fluent in Italian, but I knew that word meant *deal.*

"We do," Alessandro said, not caring about how loudly he spoke.

I cracked a cracker between my fingers and waited for them to finish. When they returned, Alessandro rocked back on his heels with his hands stuffed into his pockets and leaned against the bar.

Daddy pressed a kiss on my forehead like he cared. "Stay safe tonight. If anything goes wrong, Alessandro is with you."

"My knight in shining fucking armor." My smile dropped as soon as he stepped out of the restaurant. I leaned toward Alessandro and narrowed my eyes. "Did he tell you to fuck with me?"

His eyes glinted with amusement. "I don't know what you're talking about."

"He did, didn't he?" The cracker broke into crumbs. "Why the fuck would he do that?"

He gazed over at me with hard eyes. "Because this business isn't for women."

I rolled my eyes. "Oh, and it is for men with fragile egos, I suppose. Egos that'll get them killed." I shook my head. "I swear, if the family was run by women, we wouldn't have half the problems we have now."

He blew a breath out of his nose. "Because you'd get nothing done. It'd be gossiping all the damn time."

"What do you have against women?" I asked.

He shrugged his shoulders. "I have nothing against women. I appreciate them very much, in fact. Especially when they're on their—"

My fist clenched. "Don't finish that sentence."

Those disturbing images of Tommy getting sucked off by that whore replayed through my mind.

He chuckled and shook his head. "*Reginetta,* I was going to say when they're on their own and independent, but ..." His gaze dropped down my body for a split second. "If you want to gain my appreciation like that, I won't refuse."

I glared at him. "I bet you would like that, wouldn't you?"

There was that billion-dollar smirk again.

He stepped closer. "You would too. It'd be the first time during your whole relationship with Tommy that you actually got fucked and were satisfied, huh?"

"You think that you'd be able to satisfy me?"

He walked behind me, snaking a hand right around my neck. "Oh, *reginetta* ..." Unlike Tommy, his grip was gentle yet held so much power in it. In a single moment, his fingers could dig into my throat so tightly and make me desperate. He leaned down so his lips were against my ear. "I could do more than satisfy you."

15

chiara

ONE OF THE guys who had been flirting with me earlier stood, and I pulled myself away from him, snapping out of whatever that had been. Alessandro looked over at them, daring them to come over and say something to him.

Instead of acting tough, like they thought they were, they walked to the exit and left. Leaving me and Alessandro and a hundred bottles of liquor to ourselves.

Alessandro gazed at me like that had never even happened, then hopped over the counter, making sure not to hit his side. He grabbed a bottle of sambuca off of the shelf, pouring himself a glass.

He looked up at me. "You want one?"

"Drinking before a deal?"

He leaned over the bar, sliding my drink to me. "Between you and me, *reginetta*, your father is too strict about these deals sometimes and, hell, a bit of an annoying prick too." He clicked our glasses and swallowed back his drink.

"Why are you acting this way?" I asked, drawing my finger against the rim.

"How am I acting?"

I narrowed my eyes. "Nice? Flirty? First, you're determined to keep me away, but now ..."

He drank the rest of the contents in his glass. "I'm being *nice* to you because you have a secret, and I want to know what it is," he said. "And I think that it has something to do with that cop at your place last night." He pushed himself off the bar and headed toward the door. "I was going to tell your daddy about it ... but I thought we could keep that little secret to ourselves."

"So, you're going to blackmail me. How mature of you."

Of course he was going to use it against me. He was a *stronzo* after all. A big one too.

I followed him to the door.

"I am." He tossed me his keys. "You're driving." He winked. "In case we need a getaway driver again."

Once we got into the car, he gave me the address. We were meeting somewhere in northern Jersey. The drive was long and dreary. Alessandro was his boring self the whole time, barely speaking a word.

"Thanks for helping me out yesterday," he suddenly said, breaking the hour of silence.

I arched a brow and looked over at him.

"The Sicilian Mafia is not only after me now, but you too."

I flipped him off and turned into the lot where the meeting would be.

Once I parked in the darkest corner of the lot and cut the lights, I grabbed my purse and rummaged through it. "Who are we seeing tonight?"

"The cartel," he said, gazing in the rearview mirror, his hand grazing over the gun in his lap. "Why don't you put on that red lipstick you love wearing? Those men love something to look at."

Rain pounded against the windshield. "Is that why you brought me?"

He flashed me a smirk. "I brought you because you dug your finger into my fucking bullet hole until I agreed."

I smiled innocently at him and grabbed my lipstick. I gazed in the mirror and puckered my lips, layering it on.

A woman in heels and lipstick was a force to be reckoned with. That was what Mom had always said. And if I had to wear that all to strike a deal with the cartel, then I would. Anything for this business. Anything to prove myself to this family. Anything to get to the top.

Alessandro watched me from the passenger seat, his eyes dark and his gaze terribly inviting. He looked at me like he was thinking about something.

He eyed my shirt. "You should unbutton the top button on your shirt," he said suddenly.

I paused. "You think they would like that?" I asked, my voice nearly a whisper.

"*Sì.*"

His eyes flickered to my chest as I unbuttoned the first button of my shirt.

He clenched his jaw. "One more."

"One more?" I unbuttoned the next one, showing off a bit of cleavage.

He swallowed hard, and I pressed my knees together slightly.

Headlights blinded us through the windshield, and Alessandro snapped his head away.

Three Escalades rolled to a stop about twenty feet away from us and cut their lights.

Alessandro tilted his head and stuck his gun in his waistband. "That's our cue."

A man stepped out of the car and walked in front of it. I opened my door to step out, but Alessandro grabbed my upper arm.

"Take your gun. These guys get wild."

So, I took the gun out of my purse and tucked it away in my waistband. *Here goes nothing.*

16

chiara

JUAN GARCÍA, the man who did the cartel's dirty work, stepped out of the car with an umbrella and walked into the nearest warehouse. Rain poured down around us, and I shielded my face with my hand as it flew in all sorts of directions. About twenty of his men stood around outside of the building, guarding it from cops.

Alessandro opened the door for me and shook the umbrella out, leaving it by the door. The warehouse smelled like fish and sewer, a disgusting mixture that I would be fine never smelling again. Rain beat down outside of the rusty garage door. I walked into the room, gazing at the dozen more men from the cartel, all equipped with guns and all staring at me … the only woman here.

Juan gazed at me, lips curled into a smirk. "You brought one of the Capitelli whores for me, Alessandro?" He stood about twenty feet away, his fingers locked on to his gun.

"I'm Piero Capitelli's daughter," I said, staring blankly at him and trying hard not to get riled up from the mere thought of being associated with our family whores. I wasn't Kiara or whatever the fuck her name was.

Juan walked around me and looked me up and down like I was

a damn prize. "Capitelli's daughter?" He chuckled menacingly and turned toward Alessandro. "Did the boss make you bring her? Get her out of his hair?"

"We're here to talk business." Alessandro paused and glanced briefly at me, gaze lingering on the buttons I had popped open on my shirt. "Not *pleasure*."

Juan nodded and stepped toward me, brushing a finger against my cheek. "As long as you and I can talk *pleasure* later, *bonita*."

I slapped his hand away from my face, clenched my jaw, and said, "Don't talk to me like that. I'm not one of the whores. I'm the next Capitelli boss." Because I would be, whether anyone believed me or not.

Mom had wanted to rule beside Dad, to take a bigger role in this family, before someone killed her ruthlessly and let her bleed to death in the streets.

And on that day, I'd promised her I would follow in her footsteps.

I was up for whatever it took.

"You think your father would let a woman run the family?" Juan let out a laugh and shook his head, muttering something incoherent under his breath. He turned around and nodded to a few men, who threw three black duffel bags in front of us. "If you want to be the boss, you might want to cover your tits, *bonita*. People won't take you seriously with them hanging out like that."

All I wanted to do was tell him that I could dress however I wanted and still mean business, but then I'd look like an emotional mess, as Alessandro had suggested.

Alessandro clenched his jaw and grabbed the bags, handing me one. "Where's the rest?"

Juan waved the gun in the air. "The deal was fifty now, fifty later."

"We agreed on seventy now, thirty later, *bastardo*," Alessandro said.

Juan stepped forward, trying to intimidate Alessandro, but he didn't move an inch. Instead, he stood there, staring at Juan with the most sinister look on his face. One that even scared *me*—just a bit. It was nothing like any expression I had seen Tommy give anyone before. It was fire. It was lethal. It was so damn frightening.

Juan nodded to one of his men again. "Give him ten more."

"Twenty," Alessandro said, refusing to back down.

His fingers twitched, and I could tell he was aching to reach for his gun to shoot this *stronzo* dead right here. But we wouldn't get out alive. Not with all his men around us.

Juan pressed his lips together and shook his head. "Ten more and some information on *Mamacita* Capitelli." His dark gaze lingered on me.

Alessandro didn't even look at me, but he tensed. "Depends on the information."

A guard threw Juan another bag of money.

"There's a hit on her," Juan said.

I crossed my arms over my chest, my patience running thin. "The Sicilian Mafia," I said, shaking my head. It had to be. Even though I had changed my plates and junked my car, they knew who I was. I had been digging into their business and hanging out with their former man. "We already know that."

Juan tilted his head at me, excitement filling his brown eyes. "No. From the Capitelli family." He paused and looked between us, then at me solely. "Someone wants you dead ..." He pulled out his gun, stepped closer to me, then held it right to my head. "Willing to pay two hundred million for your head."

My heart pounded hard, but I refused to show him my fear.

The Capitelli family? Someone in my own family wanted me dead? First my mother and now ... me? Who could it be? Maybe it was the whore Tommy had been fucking with. Maybe some other whore who wanted to weaken my father or even someone who wanted me out of the way so she could have Dad all to herself.

"You kill her, and I'll kill you," Alessandro said, face void of emotion.

Juan chuckled and tipped the gun back. "The offer was tempting, but I'm not into killing women who look like you, so I passed it up. Maybe next time." He winked at me.

When he stepped back, I inhaled sharply and tried so desperately to calm myself down.

Alessandro snatched the bag of money from Juan. "Who?" he asked, a tenseness in his voice that I'd never heard before—something that I'd never thought I'd hear from him.

"That's all I know," Juan said.

After Alessandro gave him one hard stare, he grabbed my wrist and pulled me back into the car, not even bothering with the umbrella. We walked into the rain, and he threw the bags into the backseat.

"Get in the fucking car, Chiara."

Chiara …

My name had rolled off his tongue so rough, and part of me loved it. It was the first time he had said my name—my real name. Deciding not to be a total bitch now since we were in the rain and since I had found out that I had a hit on my head, I slid into the car.

Alessandro got into the car, started it, and drove for a long time before he spoke a single word. After about thirty minutes of silence, he tightened his grip on the steering wheel. "Who the fuck is after you?"

I widened my eyes at him. "You think I know? You think I walk around, knowing there's a hit on my head without having fucking protection?" I stared out the window and shook my head, watching beads of water race down the windshield. "You're a fucking idiot if you think that."

"It's because of the damn police you're fucking with," he said, angrily shaking his head. "The family thinks you're a rat."

I slammed my hand on the seat. Those were the same damn words the family had used to explain Mom's death. *She was a rat …* when she wasn't. I was sure of it. Absolutely sure.

"I'm not a rat," I said through clenched teeth.

"Then, why are you sleeping with the cops?"

I turned to face him, droplets of water racing down my chest from the rain. "Just like what you do is none of *my* business, what I do is not any of yours."

Something in his demeanor changed, and he saw a damn opportunity and took it. "So, you bribe cops with sex to get information for you? Is that all I need to do? Give you some information to get you to take the rest of your clothes off?"

Instead of scowling at him like I wanted, I stared out the windshield and laughed. "Oh, it's not like you haven't been thinking about it from the damn moment I met you." I crossed my arms over my chest. "But, unlucky for you, I don't go for man-whores."

"You went for Tommy."

"I need Tommy," I said, jaw twitching. *Don't let him get under your fucking skin.* "There's a fucking difference."

He drove down some side roads and then onto a run-down road, his hand inching closer to me every moment. "You need me too, *reginetta.*"

"And why do I need you?" I asked, suddenly starting to feel how damn wet and sticky my shirt was from the rain.

"Because I'm the only one who will take you out on business and I'm the only one who knows your little secret. I hold *your* future in my hands. I can break you, or I can make you better than your father."

I scoffed. "Why would you do that? Why would you even consider helping me?"

"Because this family is more corrupt than you think it is."

"Corruption," I muttered. *Corruption* wasn't the word I had for it. *Fucked up* sounded more like it. But this life was all I had known, and I wouldn't trade it for anything. All I cared about was getting revenge on the person who had decided to kill Mom. "If you care about corruption, you shouldn't be in this business."

He chuckled and pulled onto some dirt driveway. "I don't give a fuck about corruption. I relish in it." He gazed at me and cracked a smirk. "Maybe that's why I always find myself in your company."

17

chiara

AFTER PARKING the car behind some bushes, he nodded to the shed behind the run-down house. "We bring the money there. Five minutes, tops." He pulled the bags from the back and handed me two. "It's simple, *reginetta*. Don't fuck it up."

I took a deep breath through my nose, cursing the weather for all this damn rain we'd been getting, and sprinted toward the shed. Alessandro took his sweet time, the rain drenching his hair, making his dress shirt cling to his abs and his hair stick to his forehead.

When he unlocked the shed, I pushed the door open and walked into a heap of spiderwebs. I cowered back and scrunched my nose, bumping into Alessandro.

"Watch it," he said, locking the doors behind us.

He turned on the lamp in the far corner of the room and pulled up one of the floorboards in the very back.

Stacks of cocaine and piles of money lay under it, and my eyes widened. I glanced around the room at the floor. There must've been thousands—if not millions—of dollars here that needed to be cleaned. But at least that was what the whores were for, working at my father's strip club and cleaning the money before we used it.

I threw the bags down on the ground next to him.

"What are you doing in America?" I asked, crossing my arms over my chest and wanting to move on from his flirtatious remarks in the car. "Why are you here?"

He groaned, a thick strand of hair sticking to his forehead. "I thought you'd said that once I brought you back out, you'd stop asking questions? That was the damn deal."

After putting the wooden boards back into place, we walked back to the door. Without responding to me, he unlocked it and walked back out into the rain.

I hurried after him, right by his side the whole time. "You haven't answered any of my damn questions," I said.

I didn't know why I wanted to know more about him, but I did. There was something about him that made him different from the other men in the family, and I wanted to figure out what exactly it was.

When he reached the car, I snatched his wrist in one hand and stuck the tip of my gun right into his wound. "Why are you here?"

"Put your little toy away," he said, stopping dead in his tracks.

But I pushed it deeper into his side. He let out a guttural growl, turned around, snatched my gun right from me before I could even react, and stuck the tip of it right under my chin.

"What did I tell you?"

I didn't know what I hated more: the way he had so easily disarmed me—after the years of training I had been through—or the way I couldn't help but get excited at how damn insane this man was.

"Don't stick your nose in places it doesn't belong," he said again. "This is the last fucking time I'm going to warn you."

And because I didn't believe him, I pushed him even more. "I deserve to know."

He hadn't hurt me yet. He hadn't put a bullet through my head, like he had promised. He protected me. Over. And over. And over.

He stepped closer to me, pressing me against the car with his hips. "You're going to get a bullet straight through this pretty little head of yours if you keep asking questions, and it's not going to be by me."

"You think I'm afraid?" I asked, matching his intensity.

"You should be, *reginetta*." He ran the tip of the gun down my chest, pushing my wet shirt to the side and pressing his hips even further into me. Our clothes were soaked, yet I could feel the hardness of his cock rubbing against my stomach. "You should be fucking terrified."

And while I wasn't terrified of this side of him ... I was terrified of what I might *let* him do to me one of these days. I didn't want to fall for another unfaithful family man to get my heart broken again just because he had swooped in and saved my ass a couple of times.

I took a shaky, deep breath and pushed my hands into his chest. He stumbled back a couple of feet, cursed under his breath, threw my gun to the ground, and wrapped his hand around my throat, pinning me to the car door. His eyes were dark—pure and utter darkness. His jaw was twitching. I could feel his muscles tense against my body.

"If you think you can—"

Headlights blazed down the dirt road.

He paused mid-sentence, looked toward the light, then pulled me down behind the car and pressed a hand over my mouth. "Stay quiet."

The car parked a few feet away from ours, and he cursed, then pulled out his gun. Nobody stepped out of the car, yet he pushed me even closer behind the tire, pressing his body against mine. Someone took out a flashlight and shone it on the ground near the tires, and then ... I heard it.

Three shots to each tire. The car was behind the bushes, so the rain made it hard to see ... but they aimed and shot out each of the tires with pure ease. I had seen a shoot-out before. I had seen the aim of some of these men, but none of them were like this.

This was more than the average mafia. Not many people were this accurate, especially not when it was dark, the car was hidden behind thick brush, it was raining, and they didn't even leave their car.

I wanted to scream out in terror as two bullets whizzed right past us and hit me in the calf. But Alessandro curled his arm tighter around my waist and pressed his hand against my mouth.

"Quiet."

More bullets raced through the air, close to hitting us again. My leg felt like it was on fire, an intense pain shooting up my thigh. The blood gushed out of it, and I squeezed my eyes closed.

"Shh, shh, shh, *reginetta.*"

Someone opened the car door, and I could hear the faintest footsteps coming in our direction.

Alessandro moved me beside him, resting me against the car, and said, "Stay here."

I stared at him, wanting to do nothing more than help because I felt useless like this, but I couldn't move. With every passing moment, all I felt was more and more pain. Searing fucking pain.

How the fuck was I going to explain this to Tommy?

Alessandro grabbed my gun and crouched beside me. Two men came into view, guns pointed at the ground near us. But before they could shoot, Alessandro shot them both right in the head, killing them instantly.

He grabbed my arm, pulled me to my feet, picked me up, and hurried toward their car. Then he threw me into the backseat, started the car, and hit the gas, getting out of there as quickly as he could.

I stared at him in the rearview mirror, watching him gaze into the rearview mirror every now and then to make sure nobody was following us. He peered at me for a quick moment and clenched his jaw.

I frowned at him and said the first thing that came to mind. "Thank you."

18

ALESSANDRO DROVE for fifteen minutes on the back roads. Rain beat down hard on the windshield, and I tried so desperately to stop the blood from gushing out of my bullet wound. But the pain was quickly spreading through my leg, making it worse. He looked in the rearview mirror to make sure we weren't being followed, then pulled into the old, abandoned junkyard.

He drove by a woman sitting in a running car and held his hand up to say hello, and then he parked this car toward the back. I stared through the window at the woman, my brows furrowed. As he parked, I took off my shirt and tied it around my wound so I wouldn't bleed to death.

After Alessandro got out of the car, he opened my door and raised a brow at me being almost naked. "If you want me to fuck you, *reginetta,* all you have to do is ask."

I tried to move around to face him, but the pain shot up my leg again.

"Fuck," I cursed, taking deep breaths through my nose.

Calm yourself, Chiara. It doesn't hurt that *bad.*

I used all my strength to pull myself out of the car and land on my one good leg. Then, I tried hard to hobble out of the car to the woman's SUV—because I guessed we were just trusting random people to pick us up now.

But when I placed my foot on the ground, I almost collapsed.

Alessandro crossed his arms over his chest, the rain hitting him right on his perfect fucking face. "Does the princess need help?"

I tried not to let him get under my skin and stared over at him. "Don't push it," I said through clenched teeth. His smirk widened, and he stepped back, about to make another snarky remark that I didn't want to deal with so I said, "Please."

I hated how desperate I sounded. I hated the smug look on his face when the word tumbled out of my mouth. I hated how *I* felt when he leaned down and picked me right up into the air with his chest so close to mine, his hands touching my skin.

He placed me into the backseat of the woman's car, and I rested my leg on the seat next to me. The blonde woman hummed from the front seat, a big smile stretched across her face as she looked back and forth between us. Her makeup was done, hair pulled back into a high ponytail. I pressed my red-colored lips together and tried to forget the stupid smile she had given Alessandro when he got into the passenger seat.

Who was she? And why the hell was she picking us up again?

"Bring us to my place," Alessandro said.

"I am not going to your place." I crossed my arms over my chest. "I want to go home." So I could meet Ray and get my wound patched up. It was hurting like fucking hell, and Alessandro wanted to take me back to his place?

He reached back, placed his hand on my calf, and squeezed. Just as I had done with *his* wound a few days ago. I winced, pain shooting up my leg, and cried out.

"Hurts, doesn't it?" he asked.

I punched him hard in the arm. What was wrong with him? All I ever wanted was to go out on jobs for Dad and help the family, and all everyone wanted was for me to shut up and look pretty, pretend I wasn't hurting on the inside.

The blonde didn't say a word to me the entire time she drove us to his house. Instead, she looked back at me a few times, her gaze lingering longer than I would've liked. I rested my head back against the window, trying hard not to cry from the pain. If I had gone by myself, if Alessandro hadn't come, we wouldn't be in this mess.

Every moment, I was stuck in this god-awful car with this woman, whose perfume actually smelled good but was caked on too much, my vision blurred more and more. I could barely feel my calf, even with the immense pain. I tried hard to focus on the rain running down the car window and found my eyes closing softly.

"*Reginetta*, keep your eyes open," he said.

I fluttered my eyes and groaned. I felt like I was going in and out of consciousness, not really thinking straight. I took a deep breath and rested my head back against the window. Words started tumbling out of my mouth, words I could barely hear or comprehend myself.

"The only place you can order me around, *asshole*, is in bed," I said. And then I passed out.

———

I woke up hours later, being carried into an apartment that I hadn't been to before. The woman hurried into one of the hallways to search for something. I didn't know how much blood I'd lost, but I could see Alessandro's perfect fucking face as his brows furrowed, and there was some tension in it.

His gray eyes were searching the apartment, and I brushed my fingers against his jaw. Something about him was so … so different. I didn't know what it was. Maybe it was my severe lack of blood making me think this man was attractive.

But his skin felt good under my fingers, and I inhaled his scent and rested my head on his shoulder, trying hard to keep my eyes open. When he looked down at me, he muttered something in

Italian that I didn't understand and finally set me on the couch, propping my leg up on the white suede.

"B-but … it's going to get it bloody," I said, barely able to tilt my head up from my lying position to watch all my blood drip out. It was too difficult to even move at this point.

I tried to push myself up, but he pushed me back down.

"No," he said.

The woman came back over with some medical supplies, and I assumed she wasn't Alessandro's secret lover but a medic he had kept secret from the family. We had a doctor who could treat us—Ray—but … I guessed Alessandro needed his own. For whatever reason.

She spoke in Italian to Alessandro, and I sat there, trying to decipher what she was saying. I stared up at him, watching his neutral expression as he nodded and stared down at my wound.

"The bullet went into your calf muscle. No major arteries were hit. You're being dramatic, *reginetta*." He looked down at me with the smallest smirk on his face.

And I had the urge to hit him for calling me dramatic, but instead, I let out a low, guttural belly laugh. I clutched my stomach, the pain only making me hurt worse, but I couldn't stop laughing. Maybe it was how this whole thing was unbelievable … or that while I had been shot, now bleeding profusely and totally shirtless … I felt better than I had felt in a long time.

Alessandro's lips curled into a genuine smile, and my heart warmed at the mere sight.

19

THE WOMAN WRAPPED my leg in gauze, gave me a bottle of painkillers, said a few more words to Alessandro, and walked right out of the apartment, leaving us alone. He lingered by my side.

"Alessandro ..." I said.

He raised a brow and took off his suit jacket, which had been ruined. "First-name basis, *reginetta?* No *stronzo* this time?" He tossed his jacket onto his ruined white couch below my legs and rested my gun just out of reach on the side table.

"Do you want me to call you *stronzo*?" I asked.

"I kind of like it," he said, eyes darkening. "I like my women feisty."

"Who ever said I was your woman?"

"You did earlier with your *you only get to order me around in the bedroom* comment."

He leaned down beside me, knowing that I was unable to move a fucking inch from him and brushed his fingers down the center of my bare chest, trailing them over my cleavage in my lacy black bra. Goose bumps rose on my skin, and I shivered.

"Is that how you like to be fucked?"

"That is none of your business," I said, trying to show him that this wasn't exciting me one bit … but it was.

He brushed his fingertips lower and lower and lower until they were against the waistband of my pants. I sucked in a deep breath and kept his intense eye contact.

"Don't touch me. I have a boyfriend."

His lips curled into a smirk. "A boyfriend who's cheating on you."

My eyes widened slightly, and I pushed his hand away—even though I didn't want to. "How do you know about that?"

"Everyone knows about it. I could tell by the way he was talking with those women at the family gathering. He has no respect for you."

I pushed myself to a seated position, resting my back against the side of the couch. "And you do?"

He shrugged. "You're growing on me, *reginetta.*"

I rolled my eyes and stared at him for a long time and then I said, "So … are you going to tell me now why the whole fucking mafia is after us?"

His gaze hardened, and he immediately turned away from me, every muscle in his back tensing. I stared at him and waited a long time for an answer. And when he finally said something, I was completely and utterly shocked.

"I did rat them out," he said, jaw twitching. "But for a good fucking reason."

"You're a rat?" I said, my eyes wide.

How could I trust him? What would happen when everyone found out? Did Daddy know? Why did Dad trust him so blindly? He probably knew all of our family secrets now.

"Are you serious? You know the first thing about this business is that you don't tell anyone anything, and you ratted your family out to the fucking cop—"

"I ratted on them because they were doing shit I didn't agree with." His voice was tense, his whole body rigid.

There was something in his eyes that told me not to push it, an intense rage that actually scared me. But I pushed him anyway.

"So, drug trafficking and killing people and—"

He grabbed a glass lamp and slammed it off the table. "Like child trafficking, Chiara," he yelled. His eyes were an angry, dark mess.

My eyes widened, and I pressed my lips together. Children? They were using children?

And then I shook my head and stared right at him. "Then, why are you here?" I asked, trying so damn hard to figure out why he had come to America to start with a new family when he should be hiding out on some private island.

He had enough money. He had enough resources. Why come here, where there was danger, where he could be found by his family? And why had Dad let him into the business?

He stared at me for a long time, then turned away. "You're staying with me."

And that was the only answer he gave me, so I decided not to push it for now. I would ask him another time—when I knew I could get it out of him.

"I'm not staying with you. Tommy is probably waiting for me," I said, not really giving a single fuck about Tommy.

All I wanted from him was sweet revenge. I just had a few more fucking days to hold out to get some dirt on him. Daddy liked him too damn much for me to break his heart without him having done something to betray this family.

Even if he didn't do anything, I could always make it seem like he did.

Alessandro laughed and walked toward his hallway. "You think you have a fucking choice? After what you know now, I can't have you blabbing that to everyone, including Tommy. You'll ruin everything that I've done here."

After throwing me one last scowl, he walked into the hallway. I listened to the door close and the shower turn on.

I slumped back on the couch. One question answered, a million more I needed to figure out.

Had he told me the truth, or had he been in on such a hideous crime? How'd he get out of jail? Why was he here?

My phone buzzed, and I took a deep breath, wanting to ignore the damn thing, but it kept ringing and ringing. I growled and picked it up.

"What?" I asked through clenched teeth.

My leg began pulsing with pain, and I popped two pills into my mouth, hoping it would help.

There was some noise in the background, and I heard a door close.

"Chiara," Detective William said, his voice softer and quieter than usual. "Are you alone?" Worry was laced in his voice, and I furrowed my brows.

"Yes," I said, glancing over at Alessandro walking out of his bathroom and through his house with only a towel fixed on his hips. Beads of water rolled down the muscles in his sculpted abdomen, and I sucked in a breath.

God, how could a *stronzo* look this fucking good? It was like he was made of—

"Chiara?"

"Sorry," I said, peeling my eyes away from Alessandro, who disappeared into one of the back rooms. "Yes, I'm alone. What is so important that you had to call me now?"

"You know you have a hit on your head. And that your *friend,* Alessandro ..." He said his name with so much distaste that it sounded like he was jealous. "I heard he plans to take you in."

My heart dropped. "What do you mean, take me in?" I gazed at the man—who had put on his damn clothes—walking down the hallway toward me. My eyes flickered toward my gun on the table a few feet away, yet I didn't know if I'd be able to reach it in time.

I could barely walk with this damn leg. I didn't think I'd be able to get the gun to protect myself if William really meant what I thought he meant. He was nervous about something ... something that I couldn't quite place.

"I heard that he's going to kill you."

20

chiara

"I HEARD *that he's going to kill you.*"

As soon as the words left his mouth, I swallowed hard. Something wasn't right. Part of me didn't believe that Alessandro would kill me after he just saved me … but maybe he wanted the money. He had to get away from his family and needed money to survive. Maybe this was his only way.

He waltzed around in his gray sweatpants, his dick pressed against the front of them, and without a single shirt in sight, showing off his toned abdomen. His bullet wound was still patched up, some white gauze over it.

Instead of sparing me a glance, he pushed his hand into his pocket and walked to the kitchen. My brows furrowed for the briefest moment, and I heard William talking really fast, which he only did when he was nervous. So, I clicked off my phone and shut the damn thing off.

Alessandro started the Keurig, leaned against the counter, and looked over at me with his thick arms crossed over his chest. All I wanted to do was—

"Like what you see, *reginetta?*"

"No." *Yes.*

I lay on the couch, my tits nearly hanging out of my bra. Tonight had gone from bad (finding out someone had put a hit on my head), to really bad (getting shot by the mafia), to terribly bad (figuring out that my only hope of solving my mother's case might've been compromised). I needed something to pick me up.

"Do you have something I could wear?"

"I'd rather you walk around naked," Alessandro said, glancing down at my body.

I swallowed hard and tried so hard to think straight, think about Tommy and all the revenge I wanted to get on him, think about not being distracted by a devilishly handsome man with a thick Italian accent, standing in the kitchen in thin gray sweatpants that I could almost see right through.

"Who were you talking to?" He grabbed the coffee mug and walked around the kitchen island to lean against the wall in front of me. "Your cheating boyfriend or your cop boyfriend?"

I clenched my jaw and glared at him. "The cop, and he's not my boyfriend." I paused for a moment, listening to him chuckle, and pushed myself up into a seated position because this couch definitely made me keep slipping. No wonder I didn't buy this type of leathery shit for my apartment. "He's been compromised."

Alessandro's hand tightened on the coffee cup, his knuckles turning white. "What the fuck do you mean, he's been compromised?"

"He called me, nervous. He's never nervous. They might be tracking us. We should go."

"No," he said. "I'm tired of running. If they want to come up in here, I'll shoot them fucking dead. They won't be able to get within fifty meters of this building without me knowing about it."

So, he had people.

I grasped on to the couch for dear life, my leg hurting so terribly bad. "Do you think it's your family?"

"No, *reginetta*, it's yours." He looked so serious that I actually believed him. "The Sicilian Mafia doesn't give a fuck about the

Americans. They'd kill the police if they got into their way. They have no use for them anyway. They want us."

My mind was spinning with who would go to Officer William—the one cop who had been hunting them down for years—to find me. Tommy crossed my mind, but I shook my head. It couldn't be him. He was too damn stupid. He got followed by cops so often, and he didn't even realize it.

"Well, we have to tell my dad," I said. "He's not going to like that someone—"

Alessandro placed his coffee down on the side table and stepped closer to the couch. "That someone—his daughter—was talking to the police, and now, they know something?" Alessandro shook his head. "He really wouldn't like that," he said, mocking me.

I narrowed my eyes. "The only reason I hired that asshole was to figure out who had killed my mother because this family is absolutely useless at figuring stuff out."

"They're good at figuring shit out, but they're better at hiding it."

"What are you getting at?"

"Oh, don't be so dense, *reginetta*. I know you're smarter than that."

But … I didn't want to believe that my own family knew who had killed Mom. It was true that someone in the family had done it and that they also wanted me dead, but if they knew who had done it, they would have to risk their entire life to hide this from Dad. Because Dad would put seventeen bullets straight through the man's head when he found out.

"You're lying," I said.

"I have no reason to lie to you … except that you're annoying as fuck, you won't leave me alone, you threatened to shoot me in my exposed wound." He winked at me. "But if you ignore all those reasons, *reginetta*, maybe you'd see that I'm the only damn person in this family who is looking out for you."

21

chiara

"LOOKING OUT FOR ME?" I asked, pulling myself to my feet and staring right at him.

I didn't want to believe it, but I wasn't blind. He had been pushing me away to stay out of his business from day one because he knew that the Sicilian Mafia would come after me too. But I was too damn proud to admit it out loud, so I turned it back on him because he wasn't right in everything that he did.

"You told me the wrong address that first night so I wouldn't be able to work with you. You constantly put Tommy down and act as if I don't know what I'm doing. You led the Sicilian Mafia here and put my family at risk."

He stood inches from my face and smirked. "Are you done?"

I slammed my hands into his chest. Childish of me, I know. But he got on my damn nerves so much that I couldn't help it. "No, I'm not done."

He stepped closer to me, placing his palms on my stomach, fingers wrapping around my waist, and then he gently pushed me back down onto the couch. "You shouldn't be standing on your leg, *reginetta*. You could get hurt."

When his fingers brushed against my skin, I sucked in a deep breath. Maybe it was the medicine hitting me hard, but … something about him was so damn attractive in that moment that I didn't have a quick comeback, like usual.

He stepped closer to me and tilted his head in a demeaning manner. He eyed my calf. "Remember you had your fun with me when I got shot?" he asked, dark brown brow raised, stepping even closer to me until he stood between my legs. "It's my turn."

"Oh, so you're going to punish me now for your mistakes?"

But that didn't stop my heart from pounding harder and making me excited. Since earlier in the rain, when he had me plastered against the car, his body against mine … I hadn't been able to stop thinking about what would have happened if nobody had come and tried to kill us.

He chuckled and grasped my jaw, standing between my legs. "I only punish women for two reasons. Either they want me to or they deserve it." He stared down at me with those gray eyes. "And you, *Chiara*, deserve it more than any other woman I've slept with."

I scoffed. "I am not sleeping with you."

He reached down, his fingers brushing against the inside of my thigh. "Is that what you think?" he asked, his accent making me clench. "You think you have a choice in the matter? You won't make it twenty feet from this couch before your leg gives out."

"So, what, you're going to force yourself on me?"

He chuckled, his fingers hovering over my pussy. "No, Chiara, I won't touch you unless you want me to." He grasped my chin and made me stare up at him. "And if you want it, all you have to do is tell me."

The wetness pooled between my legs, and I gulped. All I wanted to do was scream at him to leave because I shouldn't be feeling this way about the one man who had made my life hell.

"You think I want you?" I asked, my voice tenser than I wanted it to be. From the moment the words left my mouth, he knew I wanted this more than anything—that I *needed* this more than anything. "Out of any man I could have, why would I choose you?"

"Because you're desperate for a man to please you," he said, fingers millimeters from my pussy. He slid his hand down to my throat and squeezed lightly. "Because after all the shit you've been through, you want to feel good for once in your entire life." His eyes were sultry, and he shamelessly took in my breasts in my wet bra. "All you have to do is say it, and I will give it to you."

My nipples were hard against my bra, and my pussy was pulsing.

I placed a hand on his thigh, dangerously close to his hardness. "Do I want it, or do you?"

He tensed, his jaw clenching. "Is that an invitation, Chiara?"

I swallowed hard and moved my hand over the front of his pants, my pussy clenching at how hard he was already. Alessandro growled low, placed his knee on the couch between my legs, and thrust his fingers into my pants.

"Be a good girl," he murmured down at me, his hand tightening around my throat.

He pressed his fingers against my pussy. I moaned almost instantly, needing this so bad.

He trailed the tips of his fingers down my panties and smirked. "Have you been this wet for me all night?"

I shook my head, but … I was lying. And he knew it too. He began rubbing circles.

"I think you have. Thinking about me taking you," he said, rubbing his thumb over my bottom lip roughly. "Letting Tommy be a thing of the past. It excites you."

Heat pooled between my legs. As much as I hated to admit it, it did excite me. I placed my hand firmly on his thigh and trailed it over to his cock, stroking him through his pants. All I could imagine was him inside of me, taking me any way he wanted me.

He slapped my pussy, causing me to jump, then plunged his fingers inside of me this time. "Ride my fingers," he said. "Show me how you want me to fuck you," he said in that thick accent.

I swallowed hard, my core tightening.

His palm brushed against my clit, and I closed my eyes, letting the heat build in my core. I moved my hips ever so slowly against his fingers.

"Faster," he demanded.

I moved my hips back and forth, the pressure rising in my core. The mere friction of his palm against my clit was driving me wild. I stroked him faster, feeling his cock harden underneath my hand, and moaned. He tightened his hand around my throat, and I bit my lip, trying to hold back a moan. My pussy tightened around his fingers, so close to coming. I tried to stand on my one good leg, the pressure in my core almost too much.

"Stay on my fingers," he said, holding me down so I couldn't move. "Come all over them."

I let out a small moan, my body seizing as I came closer to the most earth-shattering orgasm I'd ever had. His phone buzzed in his pocket, and he cursed. Yet he didn't move. Instead, he moved his fingers faster inside of me, curling them around my G-spot. I stroked him faster and screamed out. My legs trembled uncontrollably as wave after wave of pleasure rolled out of me.

After a few moments, he pulled away from me, his cock hard through his pants, and stormed into the other room, phone to his ear, speaking Italian. I lay back on the couch, my lips parted, my heart racing, my pussy pulsing with nothing but pleasure.

22

chiara

"PICK UP THE DAMN CALL," I said into my phone, waiting for Alice to answer.

I had gotten a whopping two hours of sleep last night, lying on this damn couch, my mind racing with everything that had happened last night. And I wasn't thinking about getting shot or that William might've been compromised.

All I could think about was Alessandro and how he had touched me, his fingers in places that I hadn't let many people touch me before. Don't get me wrong; I wasn't a prude. I just hadn't found much time since I'd found out Tommy was a big fat cheater.

The phone rang again, and I growled. Where was she?

After the fifth ring, she picked up the phone, her voice groggy. "Hello?"

"Alice, I need to talk to you now," I said, glancing into the hallway to make sure Alessandro's door was still closed. "There is something very important that happened last night."

I could hear some moving around on the other end.

"Did you finally kill that asshole?"

"No, but ..."

"Oh my God," she said, stopping me right in my tracks. "You slept with that sexy guy who kept flirting with you at the party, didn't you? What was his name again? Alex? Alec?"

"First off, his name is Alessandro," I whispered so he couldn't hear me. "And, no, we didn't do that!" But we had been damn close to it.

"But you did something, didn't you?" she asked. When I didn't say anything for a long time, she giggled like a maniac. "I knew it! God, tell me what happened. I want to know all the deets. Everything. How? When? Where? Why—actually, I know why. He's hot as—"

"Slow down," I said, glancing down the hallway again.

The door opened to Alessandro's room, and he strolled out of it for the first time since last night. His shirt was still off, his gray sweats basically plastered to his body. He walked right past me without sparing me a glance and started the Keurig for himself yet again.

"It's actually something else that I need to talk to you about."

I needed to warn her that she might be in danger. She was my closest friend, and if anyone was out to get me, they'd try to get to her first to dig up any information on my whereabouts or any incriminating information on *me*. They might even try to capture her to blackmail me.

"Are you ready to go? We have to see your father," Alessandro said, thrusting me the cup of coffee that he'd made for ... *me?*

"Hold on, Alice." I put my hand on the phone and stared at the cup. "What's this for?"

"Well, you look like shit," he said, placing the cup on the coffee table when I didn't grab it from him.

I rolled my eyes. Way to make a woman feel good.

He turned his back to me and walked into the hallway. "Maybe that's because I didn't give it to you last night, like you wanted."

I grumbled and stood, wincing at the pain in my leg. Alessandro walked into a room, rummaged through it, and then came out of it with women's clothing. I eyed it, then pulled it on, putting Alice on speaker.

"Hello?" she said through the phone. "What happened?"

"There is someone out to get me," I said, trying not to make a sound as I pulled the tight jeans over my wound. I guessed he didn't have anything shorter for me to wear, which I was actually very surprised about.

Alice was deathly quiet. And it scared me because she was never this quiet. She always had something to say.

"What do you mean, someone is after you?"

"There is a hit on my head from someone in the family," I said.

Alessandro walked back into the room, eyeing the phone. I buttoned the last few buttons of my shirt and limped to the front door, following him to the elevator.

"Has anyone been acting suspicious?" I asked, holding the phone to my ear again.

She paused. "No, not that I know of, but I'll keep an eye out."

Someone said something in the background, and I could hear the sigh in her voice as she replied, "I have to go. Stay safe. Oh, and we're going out tonight. I want to hear about your time with Alessandro."

After I hung up the phone, I slid into Alessandro's passenger seat and stared at the windshield as he drove. His hand rested on the space between us, tattoos covering his skin. He placed a hand on my knee and squeezed. "Listen to me, *reginetta*," he said, parking in front of Dad's restaurant. His hand squeezed tighter, but it wasn't a sexual action, more of a threatening one. "Don't say anything to your father about you getting shot. You're going to walk in there and act as if nothing happened. Do you understand me?"

"Why would I do that?" I asked through clenched teeth. "This mafia is going to be fucking with my family's shit now. He has to know about it."

"Chiara," he said, tenser this time, "if anyone else finds out about them, they'll be a target too. You don't want that, do you?"

"Dad will kill them before they kill us," I said, scooting out of the car and walking—trying to walk without limping—to the front entrance.

Alessandro blew out a deep breath through his nose and hurried to the entrance with me, opening the door and leaning close. "*Reginetta*, please."

I turned on my heel and smirked at him. "Are you begging?" I asked, a sudden power rushing through me. Never in a million years did I think I'd hear the gangster beg for anything. But ... I kind of liked that power I had over him.

He postured over me, then stepped back, noticing Dad in the corner of the room, watching us. Without so much as another word, he stormed past me and to him. I hurried after him this time and stood by his side, wanting Dad to know that I had been there last night and that *I* wasn't the one who had fucked this up.

Dad stood up and pulled me into a hug, like he always did, then sat back down and nodded. "How'd last night go?" he said to Alessandro but glanced at me.

What he was really asking was if I had been too much for Alessandro to handle on the assignment, not if it was successful or not. I could see it in his damn eyes and wanted to slap that expression right off of him.

"Good. Everything went smoothly."

"Any problems?"

"No," Alessandro said, lying straight through his teeth.

Dad looked at me. "Any problems?"

I glanced at Alessandro, then back at Dad. This would be my one and only chance to prove myself to the family. Prove that I wasn't going to take shit from anyone, that I could find the problematic people in the family before he could, that I could be twice the leader that he ever had been. And that started with finding Mom's killer by myself.

"No," I said. "No problems at all."

23

chiara

AFTER STARING me down for a few moments, he sat back in his seat and nodded. I took a deep breath, feeling like *I* was being interrogated, and clasped my hands behind my back. Alessandro pulled off his suit jacket and sat in front of Dad.

"We have to talk," he said to Dad. "There is a hit on your daughter's head by someone in this family."

I sat next to Alessandro and stared at Dad, watching his reaction.

"I know. I heard this morning. I have—"

"You're the leader of the fucking family, and you only found out about it this morning?" Alessandro asked.

Everyone in the entire restaurant went quiet, even me. Nobody had ever talked back to Dad. And Alessandro should've never talked back to him, especially when Dad had the opportunity to kill him in public and nobody would say a single word about it. In fact, it'd be covered up without a second thought.

I held my breath and waited for Dad to react.

Dad's jaw twitched. "Don't question me, Alessandro. I didn't bring you here to stir up trouble." He looked at me. "And that's all you seem to be doing lately."

"Are you blaming me for your shortcomings?" Alessandro asked, jaw clenching.

He had that same violent look in his eyes that he'd had last night when he killed those two men. I stared, wide-eyed, at him, wanting to tell him to calm his ass down or he wouldn't have an ass when Dad was finished with him.

Dad slammed his hands down on the table. "I'm saying that Chiara was never in danger from anyone in this family until you came to town." He flared his nostrils and swallowed hard. "I don't want you seeing my daughter again. No more assignments together. No more visiting each other's home late at night." He looked back and forth between us like he knew our secrets. "Do you understand me?"

Alessandro leaned back in his seat, kicked his ankle onto his knee, and stared at Dad. "If you're saying that I'm the one who put the hit on her head, you're lying, and you know it," Alessandro said.

"I'm done with this conversation and with you," he said. "Know your place before I have to put you into it." He glanced over at me and motioned behind me. "Chiara, Matteo will be your bodyguard. He'll be with you at all times. You won't leave his sight."

My mouth dried when I glanced up at Matteo. He was one of Tommy's friends—and by friends, I meant, one of the guards Tommy had been talking to and hanging around when he and his whore were flirting with each other at the party.

"What about my assignments with Alessandro?" I asked.

"You will have your own assignments." He slid a folder across the table toward me. "Get this done within the week," he said as if it wasn't important to the family at all.

"Chiara is safer with me," Alessandro said, standing up. "Not with some guard who doesn't know the danger she's in."

Dad stood up and glared at him. "You don't tell me how to run my family."

Suddenly, the doors of the restaurant opened, and Tommy

stormed into the room, his glare locked on me. "Where the fuck were you last night?" he asked me, voice tense.

From his eyes, I could see how angry he was that I hadn't come home to him, but he did the same thing to me every fucking night.

I parted my lips to try to calm him down, but Alessandro smirked.

"She was with me."

I rolled my eyes and sat back in my chair. Screw this. I wasn't even going to try anymore. These damn men were all hyped up on their testosterone, thinking that they could get a rise out of each other. If a damn woman ran this family, we wouldn't have this drama. We could make twice—if not three times—as much money because we would get shit done instead of … fighting like this.

Tommy and Alessandro started arguing back and forth, Tommy getting worked up for nothing. It wasn't like he was screwing a whore or anything, right? I rolled my eyes and stared at the table, trying to think of a good way to get out of this mess with this stupid bodyguard. I needed to work with Alessandro, not because he was sexy—definitely not—but because as annoying as he was, he was a decent guy.

When they started to get physical with each other, I stood and tried my hardest to stop them. I didn't need either one of them hurt, not yet anyway.

"Leave," Tommy shouted. "Chiara is mine."

I could tell that Alessandro wanted to rebut, but he didn't say anything. Instead, he leaned closer to me and said, "Don't trust anyone here. I'll see you tonight." And then he grabbed his suit jacket from the chair, slung it over his shoulder, and walked right out of the restaurant as if he hadn't just stirred up trouble for me.

Tommy angrily grabbed my hand and pulled me to the exit. Matteo followed us.

"We're going home," Tommy said into my ear, "so you'll stop being a fucking whore in front of the entire family."

24

chiara

TOMMY SLAMMED our apartment door and turned on his heel toward me, so menacingly with those savage, dark eyes. His jaw twitched, and he clenched his fists. "What the fuck were you doing at Alessandro's place?"

He stepped toward me, but I didn't step away.

"Huh? Were you fucking him? Is that what family whores like you do when I'm out working?"

"Out working?! You're never out working! You leave to fuck that damn whore every single fucking night, but I can't even associate myself with another man?!" I screamed at him, unable to hold it back anymore. "You're the biggest fucking hypocrite I know!"

"What the fuck are you talking about?"

"*Karrie.*"

Tommy shook his head at me. "You're fucking crazy. I've never cheated on you."

My eyes widened. "I'm fucking crazy?! You drive me fucking crazy! I watched her suck you off. I watched you two send naked pictures back and forth. I watched you flirt with her at the family party in front of every single one of the family members." I poked a finger into his chest. "And *you* want to call *me* crazy and a whore?!"

A look of pure wrath crossed Tommy's face, and I sucked in a quiet breath, never having seen him look so terrifying before. Not many things scared me, but the look of a crazy *stronzo* who had a loaded gun in the waistband of his pants did, especially when he'd just got outed for cheating.

"How long has it been going on?" I asked, placing a hand on my hip. All I could feel was anger and betrayal. I fucking hated Tommy, but it still hurt to know that he had betrayed me after I'd been so vulnerable for so long with him. "A few weeks? Months? Since we started dating?"

"You need to stay in your own business," Tommy said.

"Finding out that my boyfriend has been cheating on me isn't my business?"

He let out a menacing growl and stepped closer to me, wrapping a hand around the front of my throat and pushing me against the cabinets. "Don't fucking overstep. You don't know what you've gotten this family into. I know about the damn cop you're in with."

It was him. Fucking Tommy.

I shrugged my shoulders and smirked. "I don't know what you're talking about."

"Looking for your mother's murderer. Trying to bring up old fucking cases when they've been closed for years now. You need to stop before you get yourself in bigger trouble."

"I haven't been doing that," I said, lying straight through my teeth. If he could gaslight me, I was going to gaslight him. Make him feel crazy. Act like I had done nothing wrong. Because I hadn't. "I've spent all my nights doing work for Daddy or staying with Alessandro, who has given me more than *you* ever could." I scratched my nails against his chest. "Fucked me harder than you ever have. Left me begging for mo—"

Tommy squeezed my neck harder and pinned me to the cabinets. "I'm going to kill that motherfuck—"

I kneed him right in his balls and he doubled over in pain.

"That's for cheating on me." I dug the heel of my shoe right into his crotch and smirked. "That's for lying about it. And this"—I slammed all my weight onto him for a second time—"is to make sure you don't have any kids with that whore."

He turned onto his side, grasping his testicles, and I grabbed the gun from his waistband and pointed it at him.

"Get out of my fucking house," I said, jaw twitching.

Tommy crawled to the door like the stupid fucking idiot he was. "You're going to regret this."

"I'm sure I won't," I said, slamming the door behind him.

I locked it and turned back to Matteo, who stared, wide-eyed, at me.

I cocked a brow at him. "Do you want to be next? Because I'd be more than happy to put a bullet straight through your head right now for knowing about this and not keeping it a secret."

When he didn't respond, I clenched my jaw harder. "Then, get ready. I'm leaving at seven tonight for a party at Alice's."

"You're not going. I have strict orders to watch you until your father tells me otherwise."

My red lips curled into a smirk, and I stuck the gun into my waistband. I was going to Alice's damn party with or without Tommy's stupid fucking right-hand man.

25

chiara

MUSIC THUMPED through the speakers in Alice's living room.

I picked up the bottle of sambuca and took another gulp. "Fuck Tommy."

I hated that man more and more every damn day. I was beginning to think that letting him go around cheating on me wasn't even worth the fucking torture I'd endured. I should've killed him already and gotten it over with, but Dad would've minded. That fucking bastard was becoming Dad's right-hand man.

From across the room, I spotted Alessandro. Dim red and white lights lit up his striking features. I took another long sip to drown out the pain shooting up my leg and to … stop thinking about the bastard who didn't know the first thing about being part of a family. He sipped a glass and walked through the party, gaze drifting around the room as if he was looking for someone.

When his eyes landed on me, he turned my way and smirked.

"You have a free pass tonight." Alice nudged my shoulder, holding a blunt between her fingers, and directed her attention to Alessandro. "Courtesy of Tommy, who is currently out, fucking that whore."

One of the family *things* grabbed Alessandro's hand and tried pulling him on to the makeshift dance floor, but he walked past her and continued in my direction. I took another sip of the sambuca, addicted to how smoothly it went down and how much more appealing Alessandro was looking tonight because of it. Alice held out the blunt for me, but I shook my head.

Even from across the room of sticky and sweaty bodies, I could smell his licorice cologne—or maybe that was the alcohol. He was coming to me like he had last night.

I closed my eyes for the shortest moment. God, I needed a damn release. I needed more of him.

"My guard won't leave me alone," I said, nodding to Matteo standing on the other side of the room. His eyes were trained on me, and he hadn't torn his gaze away once tonight. "He's one of Tommy's friends."

Alice waved her hand in the air. "I'll take care of him." She pushed through the bodies and wrapped her arm around Matteo's bicep, flirting heavily with him.

And as soon as he looked away, I stumbled toward Alessandro, bumping into the couch, and he steadied me with a hand.

"Feeling all right, *reginetta*?"

"Feel like dancing, *stronzo*?" I grabbed his hand and stepped to him, the alcohol making me woozy.

He grasped my hips and drew me close—closer than I'd thought he would. Alessandro might be one of the most dangerous men I knew, but at least he wasn't Tommy. Tommy was an ass.

He rested his forehead against mine and smirked. "You're not supposed to be drinking on those meds."

"Care about me?" I asked, tugging on a strand of his hair.

He paused for a moment and didn't say anything, then smiled. "How'd Tommy take it when he brought you home?" he asked.

"I asked you a question, *stronzo*. I expect an answer."

I went to take another sip of the sambuca, but he took it away from me and put it onto a table.

"And I said that you shouldn't be drinking that shit right now."

I tilted my head and stared at his lips. God, they looked delicious. I wanted them on every single inch of my body. On my neck, my chest, my pussy. Until I begged him to—

"What are you doing here?" I asked, my head swaying lightly.

He pulled me closer so his hips were grinding into mine. "I came to check on you."

It was stupid, but I felt like a teenager again. Getting butterflies over the bad boy I knew I shouldn't have feelings for.

I smiled and inched my face closer, inhaling his cologne. "You do care," I whispered, my lips fluttering against his.

"I don't care about you, so don't get any thoughts in your head, *reginetta*. All I care about is keeping you safe. That's all." He didn't pull away; he pulled me closer, curling his fingers into my sides.

"Why do you want to keep me safe? Why do you keep helping me?" I asked, nose brushing against his. "Tell me …" I said, desperate to hear those words from someone's mouth who meant them.

He paused for a long moment and tilted his head closer to mine. "I don't care about you," he said, pushing his hands into my hair.

His chest was rising and falling against mine. I pressed my mouth to his, taking the damn chance because sober me wasn't going to do it.

Almost immediately, Alessandro pulled me closer, his hand tangled in my hair, his full lips on mine, tongue sliding into my mouth. "I don't give a fuck about you." He pushed me against the wall, grinding himself against me.

My hands were all over his body, sliding down his chest, disappearing into his pants. He kissed me like he had been starved and that this one little kiss did nothing for him. Like he needed more, as much as he could get.

"Fuck, Chiara, I hate everything about you," he said.

If this was what hate felt like, I fucking hated this man too.

"We shouldn't—" I started.

He dipped his head below my ear and sucked the skin softly.

"We should … back … bedroom." My words came out so incoherently that I could barely understand them myself, but he understood well.

He leaned down, wrapped his arms under my ass, and lifted me into the air, walking down the hallway and into one of Alice's spare rooms.

He kicked the door closed with his foot and tore off his shirt, lips immediately finding mine again. I backed up until my legs hit the edge of the bed and let him push me down onto it. He collapsed with me, his lips never leaving mine, and ground himself between my legs, letting me feel how hard he was for me already. And, God, I was ready for everything he was going to give me.

26

"CHIARA, I—"

Someone screamed outside the room, and the sound of bullets ricocheting off the walls cut through the air. Alessandro growled and ripped himself away from me, pulling on all his clothes. I stood up a bit too fast and grasped my head, pain splitting through it and my leg.

Goddamn. Why'd someone always have to ruin the moment between us? It was as if the world was against us fucking or some shit. But, damn, I wouldn't let that stop me. I hated that *stronzo*—really *hated* him—after that.

Alessandro peeked through the crack in the door and swore. "How the fuck do they keep sending more people? They should fucking know that I killed everyone else they'd sent."

Suddenly, his entire body tensed, and he shut the door. He grabbed my hand quite tightly and hurried to the window, opening it up. It was a two-story drop right onto hard concrete. "You have to jump, Chiara."

"Why can't we just kill them?" I asked, brows furrowed.

My guard was out there, and so were so many men from the

family. They all had guns, all had been in gunfights before. What was the difference between then and now?

"The man out in the living room is the fucker who put me in fucking prison." He looked nervous. "If you think I'm bad, you haven't seen anyone like him before. He'll torture the living fucking shit out of you."

"Are you afraid of him?" I asked, eyes wide.

He scoffed. "No, I'm not afraid of him. I'm afraid of what he'll do to *you* if he kills me," he said. "And I'm not letting you go out there to get yourself killed, Chiara, because I care about you."

My eyes widened even more, my heart racing with butterflies. Had Alessandro … had he just said what I thought he said? That he cared about me?

He pushed me toward the open window. "Don't look at me like that, *reginetta*. Jump. Land. Roll. And protect that pretty little head of yours because I don't want to clean up your cracked skull and splattered blood."

I swallowed hard, eyeing the jump, and glanced back at him. "Alessandro, I can't do it with my leg. What about Alice?" My heart dropped, and I hurried toward the door. "I need to find Alice."

He grabbed my arm, tossed me over his shoulder, and hurled me straight out of the fucking window. I screamed and grabbed on to the windowsill, trying so desperately to hold all my body weight up.

He growled, jumped out of the window next to me, hitting the ground hard, got back up, and stood under me. "Let go, Chiara. I'll catch you."

The spare bedroom door opened, and I let go before one of those men could kill me. I landed in Alessandro's arms, as he'd promised, and we tumbled to the ground together. Someone stared out the window, and bullets started flying down at us again. Alessandro grabbed my hand and sprinted as quickly and as stealthily as he could while aiming for the man's head and shooting him dead.

Everything happened so quickly. I barely knew what happened next. All I knew was that I was running through the rain of bullets to get into another car, which I assumed was Alessandro's. He started the damn car, revved the engine, and sped off into the night.

There wasn't a second thought in my mind that they'd follow us. We were bound to be followed—*had* been followed almost every time we were together now. As he drove onto the highway, he continued to look in the rearview mirror.

We got off on the second exit and sped toward a junkyard—the same junkyard we had sped into last time. He grabbed my hand and pulled me toward another car, pushing me into it and driving back off into the night—this time more stealthily.

I fumbled with my phone, about to text Alice to see if she was okay, when Alessandro grabbed my phone and hurled it right out the window and onto the highway.

"Don't call. Don't text. Don't contact anyone."

"But Alice ... what if she—what if they take her?"

"Does she know anything about me? Anything about the family business?" he asked, jaw twitching.

I gulped. "Nothing about you. Some about the family business."

After a few moments, he blew out a deep breath. "She should be fine."

"Should be?!" I nearly screamed at him.

This man had the damn nerve. She was either endangered or she wasn't. And either way, I needed to make sure she was okay. She hadn't been in any shoot-outs as far as I knew. She was one of those *let the guys do all the dirty work* kind of girls.

"Sit back and shut your mouth," Alessandro said. "Be thankful you got out alive."

27

chiara

I STORMED into Alessandro's apartment. This would be the first place anyone would probably look for us, *if* they knew where he lived. He walked in after me and shut the door, his footsteps making my heart race.

"What is wrong with the damn princess now?" he asked, tension in his voice. "I saved your ass again, and you're still angry with me."

I turned on my heel. "Do I have to remind you?! You threw me out a second-story window! Threw my phone onto the highway! And refused to let me see if Alice is okay!"

"She's fine," he said.

His phone was sitting on the counter, buzzing over and over. He threw his jacket down and turned it over, rolling his eyes when he saw the sender. Instead of answering any of the messages, he threw it back down and turned to walk down the hall.

When I heard his bedroom door close, I snatched his phone and started going through the messages. Maybe I could call Alice. All were from Dad, who was asking if we were okay. I had the urge to answer it, but I refused. I didn't need his drama in my life right now.

I loved him with my entire heart, but … I needed a break from him.

As soon as we saw him, he'd probably go off and ask why the Sicilian Mafia was trying to kill both of us now, say how someone in their family had put the hit on my head and *not* anyone from our family … because he trusted everyone under him.

Alessandro snatched the phone away from me and put it back on the counter. "You're hell-bent on getting yourself in trouble, aren't you?" he asked, moving closer to me.

I took a step back and bumped into the counter. He placed his hands on the counter, his arms trapping me.

The phone buzzed again, nearly falling off the counter. But he ignored it and stared down at me, his eyes a stormy gray, muscles swollen under the dim kitchen light.

My breath hitched. "Aren't you going to get that?"

He inched closer to me, dipping his head so his nose brushed against mine. "No."

"It's my father," I said.

This fucking man. I didn't know if I wanted to rip his clothes or his head off for being such a dick all the damn time. But I needed some time to think about what had happened.

"I don't give a fuck who it is," he said, pressing himself to me. "I'm sick of these damn interruptions."

He wrapped his hand around my throat and pulled me closer to him, forcing me to stare up into his eyes.

I could feel him through his pants, could feel my nipples pressing hard against my shirt, could feel his hands all over my body, like they had been a few hours ago.

"You're mine now."

And when he kissed me hard on the lips, I kissed him back, wrapping my arms around his neck. Desperate to kiss him. Desperate to touch him. Desperate for him.

In that moment, like some sort of magical fairy tale, everything just melted away. All my worries. All the drama. Everything. And it was just us.

He tangled his hands into my hair and pulled me back by it hard, peppering kisses down my neck. He slipped his hand into my pants and dragged his fingertips against my folds, then pushed them into me.

"You're so fucking wet for me." He sucked on my neck, lips trailing over my collarbone. "You want me to finally fuck you, Chiara?"

I let out a breathy moan and nodded. "Oh God, please."

"Show me," he demanded in my ear.

I swallowed hard, my pussy tightening. His palm brushed against my clit, and I closed my eyes, letting the heat build in my core. I moved my hips ever so slowly against his fingers.

"Fuck, you can go faster, baby." He rubbed his thumb in circles on the sensitive bud. "Faster."

I moved my hips back and forth, the pressure rising in my core. The mere friction against my cunt was driving me crazy. He pressed his lips on my soft spot, and a wave of pleasure rolled through me. Without another word, he slipped off my shirt and pants, as if he was desperate for me too.

I snatched the collar of his shirt and fumbled with the buttons, yanking it off, then my hands traveled over his bare abdomen and chest, feeling all the thick muscle underneath.

Before I could stop myself, I pulled his hand from my pussy, twirled around, and rubbed my ass against his hard cock.

"Please, I can't wait any longer." I never begged, but it seemed like I couldn't stop right now. All I wanted was for him to be inside of me, thrusting himself deep, filling me completely.

He growled in my ear, one hand slipping around my waist and rubbing my clit again, the other pulling one of my legs up into the air. He undid his pants, pulled them down, and then positioned himself at my entrance, rubbing the head of his cock against my wet pussy.

"Fuck, I've been imagining what you'd feel like." He pushed himself inside of me, filling me up inch by inch, fingers rubbing quickly against my folds, driving me higher and higher. When every inch of him was inside of me, he stilled and groaned, "Tighten your fucking pussy."

My walls clenched around him, and I bucked my hips against him.

He trailed his hand up to my breast and squeezed harshly, rolling my nipple around his palm and sending another wave of heat to my core. "These fucking tits," he groaned against me.

I bit my lip, trying to hold back a moan. When he took my nipple between his fingers and tugged harshly, I couldn't stop the moan from escaping my throat. My pussy tightened around his dick, the pressure too high in my core.

"Stay on my fingers," he said, holding my hips in place so I couldn't move. "Come all over me."

I let out a small moan, my body seizing as wave after wave of pleasure rolled out of me. When I came down from my orgasm, he turned me around, wrapped his arms under my legs, lifted me up into the air, and walked with me toward the floor-length windows in his living room. I could see all of the city from here, all of the cars below, all of the lights on in the other buildings downtown.

"My turn," he said into my ear.

He started to pump into me, holding me into the air and using my body for his pleasure. My breasts bounced slightly. I loved the feel of his cock inside of me. I couldn't wait for it any longer. I started begging. Begging for him to fill me up. Begging for him to come inside of me. Begging for him to fuck me all night long.

"Please, Alessandro," I mumbled. "Fuck me harder. God, I need it."

He tossed me onto the couch, crawled up after me, and slid himself between my legs again. He moved his hips quickly, so skill-fully, hitting my G-spot every time, and kissed me.

My breasts bounced against his chest, my fingers digging into his shoulders. "More," I whimpered into his chest. "Give me more."

He groaned against my lips, his hand sliding to my throat, and stilled, giving me everything I'd ever wanted.

28

chiara

MY FINGERS BRUSHED against his shoulder, the moonlight flooding in through the windows and hitting his sculpted back. I dragged my nails against the muscles and sighed into his shoulder. He stared at me and brushed a strand of hair from my face.

"So …" I said quietly.

Something about being in his bedroom with him, about seeing him calm and collected rather than that guarded man I'd seen these past few weeks … it made me feel … warm.

Before I could say anything else, he cleared his throat. "We're not together."

I pressed my red-stained lips together and glanced down between us. "I didn't want to date you anyway," I said.

I didn't like Alessandro. Not at all. He was just attractive. That was all. Someone to fuck when I needed to relieve some stress. Definitely NOT boyfriend material. And plus, even if he were, I couldn't get into a relationship now.

After a few moments, he got out of bed and retrieved his phone from the kitchen. I grabbed one of his oversized T-shirts from the edge of the bed, pulled it on, and closed my eyes, resting my head against the headboard. My chest tightened, and I didn't know why.

There was definitely nothing between us.

There couldn't be.

Not in this business.

Not when I had my dickhead ex-boyfriend to take care of.

Alessandro appeared at the door with his phone to his ear. "Hello?" he asked.

Someone yelled on the other end of the phone, and it sounded like Dad. It was so damn loud that I could hear him all the way from the bed.

He pulled the phone away from his ear, put it on speaker, and started to go through his closet.

Dad's voice came through. "… business in New Jersey, at the location I sent to your phone."

"When?" Alessandro asked, refusing to meet my gaze.

He shifted through some ties, and I sucked in a deep breath, watching his back muscles flex. This feeling was nothing but physical.

"Tomorrow. Four in the morning." Dad grumbled something inaudible. "Is Chiara there with you?"

Alessandro glanced at me, and my heart raced. "No."

"Good. Don't tell her. She's too uptight about shit like this."

My eyes widened, and I glared at the phone. Uptight? The only one uptight was him.

"Who'll be there?" Alessandro asked.

"Just you," Dad said.

Dad wanted him to go out alone on a solo mission? I didn't like the sound of that. What if Alessandro got put in a—

Stop it, Chiara. You don't care about him like that.

"I need you to leave tonight," Dad said over the speakerphone.

Alessandro glared at it, his face void of any emotion about what we'd done. I pulled the blankets over my body and stared up at him, wondering how he'd respond.

Why was this so sudden? Didn't he think there were bigger

things to worry about now that the Sicilian Mafia had started a war on Dad's land? He wanted Alessandro, our biggest asset, to leave?

Something didn't feel right in the pit of my stomach, yet nothing ever felt right in this family. We did as we were told. No questions asked. That was how it had always been since I'd been a child and Mom was still alive.

Without another word, Alessandro shut the phone off and said something in Italian that I didn't quite understand. Then, he pulled out a duffel bag and tossed some clothes and essentials inside of it.

"You're really going?" I asked.

He gave me a chilling look. The real Alessandro was back.

Cold. Mean. Cruel.

I didn't know if I'd ever see that vulnerable, passionate side of him again. We had gotten this *thing* out of our system. We wouldn't need each other anymore. We wouldn't crave each other anymore. It was over between us.

Over.

"Of course I'm going to go," he said, grabbing his gun and stuffing it into his waistband. "It's work."

"It doesn't feel like work. It feels like he's trying to get rid of you."

"So, what, Chiara? *You* care about *me* now?" he asked. Something in his voice sounded so desperate, as if he wanted me to say so, as if he needed me to tell him that I did care about him.

But ... was that what this was? Did I care about him? Could I care about him?

"Don't flatter yourself." I found myself saying without even meaning to. At my admission, he looked sort of ... upset.

As quickly as the emotions crossed his face, they were gone. He snatched his bag off the bed and stormed to the bedroom door.

I didn't know what possessed me to do it, but I hopped off the bed—dressed only in one of his oversize T-shirts—and hurried after him. Just as he was about to walk out the door, I grasped his wrist and forced him to turn back to me.

He spun on his heel, eyes wide and wild. "If you don't—"

Before he could finish his sentence, I wrapped my arms around his neck and kissed him hard on the lips. It wasn't want or desire or even lust. This man … this man had constantly sought out ways to protect me even if I was disgustingly rude to him.

When I pulled away, my heart was racing in my chest. His facial features softened, hard gray eyes melting. I gently let my hands glide down his chest, feeling all the hard muscle underneath.

"I do care about you," I whispered and swallowed hard. "I don't know why, but I do."

A million different emotions crossed his face.

I waited and waited and waited for him to say something. To say *anything* in response.

Instead, he rested his hands on my hips. "Be careful with your guard when I'm gone."

Then, without saying goodbye, he tossed me the keys to his apartment and walked out the front door.

29

alessandro

FUCK CHIARA.

I fucking hated her. I hated the way she trusted me so much. I hated the way she knew exactly what she was doing. I hated that I'd told her I cared about her. I hated how I felt about her. I hated that I couldn't stop fucking thinking about her.

There was only one other time I'd felt like this. With Bella. The whore who had cheated on me with my brother, who told me I knew too much in the family, who sold me out for ratting on the Sicilian Mafia for trafficking.

She was the daughter of the don, and she had put me in fucking prison.

I gripped the steering wheel and slammed my fist into the dashboard with the other.

Why the fuck did I feel so fucking good when I was with Chiara? Why had I let my guard down? Why did I want her approval more than anything?

Rain beat down on the windshield as I veered onto the highway, heading for New Jersey.

When she had told me she cared about me … God, all those memories of Bella had flooded my memory. I didn't want to end up back in that shithole they called prison. I didn't want to die in the hands of the Sicilian Mafia. I didn't want to lose Chiara.

But I had no other choice. I was so damn close to piecing everything together. There was a reason I had come to New York, and there was a reason I'd chosen to weasel my way into this family. That reason wasn't Chiara … but maybe that was why I'd stayed here for so long.

I could've found out everything that I needed already, but I refused because Chiara would be caught up in the mess. So, I stayed around and helped her when she was in danger. Because I was the one who'd put her in danger. And I wouldn't let anything happen to her.

Ever.

After two whole hours of trying to get her out of my mind and failing miserably, I pulled up to the address her father had sent me. The lights were off, no cars in the driveway. I waited on the other side of the road and cut my lights. It was the middle of the night, and nobody was home.

Something wasn't right.

I rested my head against the headrest and blew out a deep breath. My phone buzzed in my pocket, and I knew it was Chiara without even pulling it out of my pants. I ignored the call, not wanting her to mess this job up tonight.

Once the phone stopped buzzing, I pulled it out and glanced at the screen.

A missed call without a voicemail and a text.

Chiara: I hope you don't mind me staying the night.

Me: I gave you the keys for a reason.

Chiara: Don't need to be so rude about it.

My lips curled into a small smile, my chest tightening. But as quickly as the smile appeared, I forced it away. Nope. I was *not* feeling like this about her. I could like her. I could protect her. But I wasn't going to lov—

A car pulled into the driveway, and I sat up taller, thrusting my phone into my pocket and snatching my gun from my waistband. Time to get this shit over with.

30

alessandro

IT WAS A CLEAN JOB. At least, I thought it would be.

I watched the man walk into his house. I followed him. I told him the consequences of not paying up to the family. And when he thought about running, I tied him down to his kitchen chair, lit a cigar for him, and stuck it between his lips.

"This might hurt," I warned, not giving a fuck if it actually did.

All I wanted was to make this quick and get back to Chiara. I didn't trust that guard of hers to not try something. She was smart, but she trusted the family a bit too much.

In this business, you were never safe.

There were always people out to kill you.

It didn't matter who you were.

After taking my time preparing in the kitchen, I laid three knives, all in different sizes, in front of the man. One santoku. One chef's knife. One cleaver, my favorite of all of them. Sadistic? You could call it that. But it was the most fun for this job.

"Which one?" I asked, pointing to them.

The man's eyes widened, his lips trying to move with the cigar still in his mouth, as he shook his head from side to side, sweat dripping from his forehead.

When he made no coherent words, I smirked at him. "None?"

He nodded and looked relieved when I pushed them to the side of the table. Then, I pulled out a set of pliers from my bag and showed them to him.

"These will have to do," I said, grabbing one of his tied hands and grasping his pinkie fingernail between the pliers. "It'll be quick."

Again, his eyes widened, and he choked on his own spit, shaking his head furiously.

I clamped down on the nail. "Painless."

His face turned red.

I ripped off the first nail. "Easy."

He screamed out, the cigar dropping from his lips. I set the bloody nail on the table beside him, grabbed the cigar, and pushed it between his lips again.

"Next time you drop this, it'll be your finger."

After spending the next ten minutes finishing the job, I gathered the nails and pushed them toward him. "I'll leave these as a warning for you next time. Pay up when we ask. We've helped you and—"

"Drop the gun and turn the fuck around," someone said, muzzle of their gun against the back of my head.

I pressed my lips together and clenched my jaw. Fucking hell. I should've fucking known. I should've stayed with Chiara, told her father to suck it, and left for good. Gotten out of this shit before anyone had a chance to throw me back in prison for their wrongdoings. But I was so close—so fucking close.

"I said, turn the fuck around."

After pushing my gun from the table onto the ground, I turned around to face the one and only Tommy. All I could see was rage in his eyes, the look of a boy who thought he was a man because he had a gun.

"I told you if you didn't stay away from Chiara, this would happen, didn't I?"

My lips curled into a smirk. "Chiara?" I asked, trying to rile him up. "Don't know who that is."

He growled and pushed the muzzle right between my eyes. "My girlfriend."

"You mean, *reginetta*." I grinned wider and stared him right in the eye. I wasn't afraid of dying. I had seen too much shit in this lifetime, but I wasn't going to let a cheater, a liar, a boy, pull the trigger and kill me.

"What happened between you and her?"

"Does someone have their feelings hurt?" I asked. "Feelings and business don't work well together, *Tommy boy*."

"I asked you a fucking question," he said, his hand shaking in rage, jaw twitching wildly.

"Between us?" I chuckled and stepped closer to him, feeling the metal against my forehead. That was when I saw it … the others with him. There were four, five at the most, inside the house with their guns pointed at me. I swallowed hard and tried not to let it get to me. "She caught feelings for me. Asked me to fuck her last night. Knelt at my feet, begging for me to thrust my cock down her throat."

Tommy let out a vicious growl, and I chuckled again. What a weak guy. Getting all bent out of shape because his ex-girlfriend had slept with me after he had been cheating on her for weeks upon weeks.

The next words actually hurt me to say—I didn't want to say them, but I had to say them. Tommy was a prick, a bigger prick than my brother, and deserved all the shit I was about to give him for cheating on Chiara.

"She's a whore, Tommy, just like the ones you sleep with behind her back." I grinned. "But she's only a whore for me. My little slut who'll do anything I ask her to do. Get on her knees. Suck my cock. Let me fuck her in *your* bed."

Instead of pulling the trigger, Tommy punched me straight in the face. I went for his gun, but there was more than him in the room now with us. There were at least five other guys from the family, all there to make sure things went smoothly, their guns trained on me.

I was trapped. And if I didn't think of a way to get out of this, I'd be dead soon.

31

alessandro

BAG OVER MY HEAD. Hands tied behind my back. Tape over my mouth. I sat in the back of the car between Tommy and another man from the family. The blood trickled down from my nose and onto my shirt.

I'd buy another one—if they didn't kill me.

All I wanted was to ask why I was really here, but I already knew. I had overstepped before they trusted me. I shouldn't have gotten involved with Chiara and her troubles … but I couldn't help myself. All my life, I had been used, either by the mafia or by the whores in it.

But Chiara … Chiara was different.

Chiara wanted nothing to do with me, and that was what I liked about her. She didn't need a knight in shining armor. She had all her shit together already, knew what had to be done before it needed to be done, stuck her nose in places she wanted it to be to figure stuff out.

She was strong. Independent. Didn't need me.

But, damn, did I want her.

The car stopped, and they pushed me out of it, dragging me by my shirt collar because I couldn't walk with my feet tied together. The gravel turned to grass, and the grass turned to concrete under my feet.

This time around, I didn't know if I'd be able to get out of this.

I hated how close I had been to figuring it all out. I needed a bit more evidence.

Someone locked the cuffs around my wrists to a chain overhead, my entire body hanging from it. When they finally pulled the bag off my head and I could see again, I stared at Chiara's father and the don of the Sicilian Mafia. Together, with at least twenty other family members, standing guard with guns, in a concrete basement some-where—I assumed Chiara's family house.

And at that moment, all my suspicions were confirmed.

Chiara's family was trafficking children, doing hell knew what to them—selling them off, raping them, doing god-awful things that I didn't want anyone to ever think about, things that I had witnessed long ago in Italy.

So many disgusting and bad memories were rushing through my head because … I had been one of those kids. I'd found my way out of that shithole, found my real family, entered this life so no other child would ever have to deal with that shit.

I wanted to stop it.

Now, I was about to die for it.

"It's nice to see you again, Alessandro," Ricinni, don of the Sicilian Mafia, said. He walked around me, looking me up and down.

All I wanted to do was lunge at him, kill him, torture the shit out of him, like I'd wanted to do before I was sent to prison. But I'd never had the chance to get close enough to him toward the end.

They started talking to me, but I didn't listen. It was all nonsense. Total and utter bullshit. I'd figured everything out about this family. It didn't matter if they killed me now. I knew the truth, and I hoped Chiara would find it out soon too.

After an hour of hanging there, refusing to speak, not listening to what they were saying, not admitting shit to them, they started the torture. Hitting me as hard as they could until my back was bruised beyond belief. Sliding a knife through my flesh and making me numb to the pain.

None of it hurt as bad as what I had endured in this life. None of it mattered.

Another hour passed. Blood gushed from multiple wounds in my abdomen, from my nose. I could barely see out of my right eye from the swelling. Everything hurt, yet all I could think about was Chiara.

Her smile when she'd looked at me last night and I told her I cared about her. Then the frown she had given me this morning when I told her we weren't together and how she brushed it off as if it were nothing.

All I wanted was to see her again. One last time.

Chiara's father's fist collided with my jaw. My vision blurred. They asked me what I knew even though they already knew. I shook my head back and forth. They asked me who I was working for. I spat the blood back into their faces. They picked up a phone and dialed a number, put it on speaker, and let me listen.

"Hello?" Chiara's voice came from the other end.

I lifted my head enough to look at the phone. I tried to speak, but nothing would come out.

"Sweetheart," her dad said, looking straight at me, "I have some business I want you to take care of tonight—cartel business. Be at the river at one a.m. Don't be late. Prove to me that you can lead this family." And then he clicked off the phone and smirked at me. "Tommy," he said, staring me in the eye and nodding toward the door.

My heart dropped, and I gathered all the strength I had in me to scream at him not to. "No!" I screamed. "Don't touch her."

But it was too late.

Tommy was gone. He was going to kill Chiara.

32

chiara

I DIDN'T EVEN WANT to go on this stupid fucking mission. Dad had tried to make it seem like it was supposed to be important. Get the rest of the money from the cartel and hide it somewhere. But it wasn't that much money—at least not as much as last time—and my guard was here, watching my every fucking move.

We sat in the car in the same place we had been last time, and I stared through the windshield at the empty garage, waiting for the cartel to finally show up. The time on the car read *12:45 a.m.* Fifteen minutes until they were supposed to be here.

I wrapped my hand around the steering wheel and blew out a deep breath. I had texted Alessandro three times today, asking where he kept all his shit in his house, but I really wanted to know if everything was all right and when he'd be back.

I didn't know why I had this little obsession with him. I didn't want to be involved with another mafia man. I wanted something simple and easy outside this family. Someone to go out on dates with, someone I didn't have to keep my shit together with, someone I could love.

But … something drew me to him.

He hadn't gotten back to me all day, and I didn't know if something was wrong. Maybe I was too overbearing. We weren't in a relationship. He'd said that he didn't want one with me. But he cared at least.

What if something was wrong? What if something had happened in New Jersey last night? What if the Sicilian Mafia had found him and was bringing him back to Italy and I never saw him again?

My chest tightened. I didn't want to never see him again. I wanted to see him now, hear from him now. I wanted something to tell me that he was okay.

Yes, I was falling for him even though he got on my every last nerve.

It was hard to admit, but here I was, admitting it to myself.

My phone buzzed in my pocket, and I pulled it out quickly, hoping it was him. Dad's name glared on the screen. He never called this late.

I took a deep breath and tried hard not to sound pissed off when I answered it. "Hello?"

"Chiara, are you at the meetup point?"

"Yes, Dad."

"What's wrong?"

I clenched my fist. "Why don't you believe in me?"

He paused for a long time. "I do believe in you, Chiara."

"So, what's your reason for calling?" I asked, watching the road to see if any cars were approaching. But there were none. "Why're you calling me in the middle of a job?"

"I've been thinking of your mother lately," he said.

I listened to some glasses click on the other side of the phone, and I knew he was drinking. He always drank when he thought about her.

My heart sank at the mention of her name, and I glanced down at the steering wheel. Mom. I missed Mom too.

He paused for a second. "Know that I love you."

I curled my lips into a frown. "I love you too."

His voice sounded gruff. "I'll talk to you later."

Then, there was more clinking of glass and some shuffling, and then the phone went dead. Something inside of me didn't sit right. I stared down at the phone and frowned even more. He never called me like that, never said he loved me and sounded like he meant it.

A car raced down the street, and I pushed my phone into my pocket. They were here.

Whatever it meant, it would have to wait.

The car pulled up in front of us, and I squinted at it. Two cars, a handful of men at the most. It wasn't anything like what I'd experienced last time. Last time, there had been at least five cars with so many more guards. Something was wrong. Something was very, very wrong.

I stared through the glass, and my eyes widened. There wasn't just anyone in the other car.

It was Tommy.

33

alessandro

CHIARA'S FATHER sat across from me, knocking back a glass of scotch. My vision was blurring, my head feeling light, and all I could feel was pain. Everything hurt, but my heart hurt worse. They were going to kill her. They were going to take her away from me, like they had taken everything away from me when I was six.

Six.

I had been a damn kid then, and I felt like one now because I was helpless.

I couldn't help Chiara, no matter how hard I tried.

"You're disgusting," I said through clenched teeth. "Ordering a hit on your own daughter."

He chuckled and knocked back more alcohol. "Who says she's going to die tonight?"

"You order a hit on your wife too?" I asked, blood dripping from my mouth. "You wanted to kill her because she knew the man you really are, what kind of business you're really in, that you abuse ch—"

With a set of brass knuckles, he hit me hard in the face again. My head bounced around, and darkness slowly filled my vision, but I fought it as hard as I could. I wouldn't let him kill Chiara. I couldn't let him kill Chiara.

"You care too much about her," he said. "You know too much. You aren't getting out of here tonight. Chiara will prove herself and kill you for everything you know."

My heart sank in my chest. *What a sick fuck.*

That was what he wanted me to believe. I knew it wouldn't happen, and if it did, he'd be waiting to kill her too right after I was dead. Chiara knew too much about him. She'd dug when he told her not to dig. If she got out of this alive, she'd be one hell of a don.

chiara

This was all a setup. Everything about this was a setup. From the moment Dad had called, I had known something was up. And now? Now, I was trapped with my stupid fucking guard in the passenger seat, Tommy in front of me, and a boatload of mafia men who wanted the money for my head.

I pretended like I didn't know a thing. What was I going to do? How was I going to get out of this? I didn't have enough bullets in my gun to kill them all. I had to get out of here, and I had to get out of here now.

"Chiara," the guard said to me from the passenger seat.

He stared at me, waiting for me to respond, but there was a look in his eye that told me it was over. I was going to die tonight.

I blew out a deep breath and nodded to the SUV in front of us, still blinding me with its headlights. If I went for my gun, I knew he'd try to kill me. There was no escaping unless …

"Maybe I should change my shoes before we get out," I said, staring down at my red bottoms. "I don't want to get them dirty. They look kind of dangerous."

He paused, brows furrowing together for a moment. "That's not neces—"

I yanked my heel off my right foot and stabbed him right in the eye, shoved the heel as deep as it would go. He reached for his gun, pointing it right at me and fumbling with the trigger. I grabbed the barrel with my bare hand and forced him to point it right at him before he could pull the trigger.

The sound of a gunshot echoed through the night. A bullet went straight through his head, blood splattering everywhere, including on me. I hit the accelerator and sped out of this damn place.

But it was no use. Tommy was on my ass with his goons. People were shooting at the car, breaking the back windshield, glass flying everywhere. I sped through the city. All I could feel was adrenaline and pain, heartbreak that Dad had set this up.

Even if he hadn't set this up … Tommy would kill me tonight for what I had done to him the last time I saw him. He would kill me, hide my body, and take the money from whoever had posted the reward.

One of my tires blew out. Then another, then another. I cursed and prepared for the absolute worst. I grabbed the gun, made sure I had mine, and sprinted out of the car as it came to a complete stop.

Bullets still rained down around me, and I dodged them as best as I could, sprinting to the only place where I knew I had extra ammo and more guns. My apartment.

34

chiara

IT MIGHT'VE BEEN stupid to go to my apartment, but I had nowhere else to go. Alessandro's place was across the city, and I wouldn't be able to get there in time before someone shot me dead. I swallowed up my fear and hurried down the back alleyways toward my apartment.

Tommy knew exactly where I was headed, so I couldn't take any detours.

After taking a deep breath, I willed my legs to move faster and faster. The bullets had stopped whizzing past my head, and I knew I had moments before they started back up again. We were in public, and while we had bought some of New York's finest cops, the city wouldn't allow the killing of an innocent woman in the streets by the mafia.

But even knowing that, I didn't believe it.

Cops had killed people in broad daylight and gone without repercussions.

When I saw my apartment building, I hurried inside and took the stairs two at a time until I reached my apartment door. I wasted no time unlocking it, rushing inside, and putting the dead bolt on it.

After I pulled up a floorboard in my bedroom for the ammo, my heart dropped. Tommy must've come back and taken it all out. He must've known that this was going to happen, had planned for me to come here so he could kill me.

Oh my God.

Oh my fucking God.

Someone pounded on my door and then blew the locks right off it. I hid in the closet and prayed to God that they wouldn't find me even though I knew they would. Tommy would find me, kill me, and reap the rewards.

I closed my eyes, grasped my guns to my chest, and thought about Mom. About her smiling face. About how I would see her soon. About how I'd never found the answers that I had been looking for … or maybe I had. Maybe these were all the answers I needed.

Dad was a liar.

Dad was a snitch.

Dad had killed Mom. Like he was about to kill me too.

The door opened, and I listened to footsteps entering my apartment. How many had I killed? Had I killed any while I was on the run? I must've killed at least a few, or they were still outside the door, waiting for us to come out.

I didn't know how many bullets I had left. All I knew was that one gun was loaded, and the other was almost empty. I stayed as quiet as I could until someone opened the closet door. Then, without thinking, I fired off a shot, killing the guard instantly.

More began to file into the room at the sound of a fired gun. I put bullet after bullet into their bodies, trusting that my aim was good enough to kill the men. When another one came into the room, I tried to fire off another bullet, but the gun was empty.

I swallowed hard and stumbled back as Tommy walked into the room. Gun drawn and pointed at me, he had the evilest smirk I had ever seen.

"You wanted to be a whore while I worked? Going out with

Alessandro. Thinking you were slick, Chiara. Thinking you were such a big girl in this business."

He stepped toward me, and I stepped back, bumping into something and falling back onto my ass. I posted my hands behind me and scurried back until my back hit the wall.

This was it. This was the end.

Tommy took the safety off the gun, crouched down to my level, and put it right against my head. "You don't know shit about this family. And what you do know is too fucking much. Your daddy wants me to bring you back so he can kill you himself, but I want to do it. Just like my father killed your mother."

My heart dropped. Fear and anger and heartbreak ran through every part of me. Tommy's family had killed Mom. Tommy's *father* had killed Mom. Mom was dead because of my ex-boyfriend.

I balled my hands into fists, but I couldn't move. It hurt so fucking bad.

"We're supposed to keep her alive," the only other living guard said to Tommy.

Without even looking in his direction, Tommy shot him straight through the fucking head. The guard fell back against our bedroom room wall, his blood splattering everywhere.

I fucking hated him with everything I had. I wished I hadn't been so stupid. I wished I'd killed him when I had the fucking chance.

Why'd I wait? Why'd I want revenge so bad?

Tommy pushed the gun against my forehead. "*Ciao*, Chiara."

And then the sound of a gun firing off rang through the entire apartment.

35

chiara

TOMMY DROPPED HIS GUN, blood spurting from the giant hole in his hand. I stared, wide-eyed, at him, grabbed his gun from the floor, and pointed it at whoever had shot him. I prayed to God it was Alessandro, back from New Jersey, but instead, it was Tommy's whore of a girlfriend.

She furrowed her brows at me. "What are you waiting for? Kill his ass."

Confused, I looked back and forth between Tommy and her. What the fuck was going on? Why was she here, and why was she helping me kill him? Didn't she want his dick all the fucking time?

Tommy lunged at me, and I shot a bullet straight through his abdomen. Then another through his head. Then another. And another. And another. Until all the bullets were gone and I was standing over him.

He lay in a pool of his own blood on our bedroom floor, too many holes in his head for me to count. I threw the gun down at him and told him to fuck himself, looking back up at his whore and getting ready to strangle her.

She gave Tommy the most disgusted look she could muster. I

turned to her and stalked forward, snatching her gun right out of her hand and pointing it directly at her.

"Why the fuck did you shoot him?" I asked through clenched teeth.

It didn't make sense. None of it made any sense at all. She shouldn't be here.

"You won't believe me if I told you," she said, staring right at the muzzle, then at me. Jaw clenched, hair pulled back into a tight ponytail, dressed in something a lot more comfortable than her usual whorish clothes.

"You're right," I said, pushing the gun against her forehead. "I wouldn't."

"If you kill me, you will never find Alessandro."

"Don't speak his name like you know him," I said through clenched teeth, my entire body shaking. "You're not going to take him away from me either. He's mine, and your whore hands aren't going to touch him."

She scrunched up her nose. "You think I wanted Tommy? I had to do what I had to do for Alessandro. I needed to get all the information out of Tommy's sorry ass."

"You work for Alessandro?" I asked, unable to piece this all together.

Her gaze flickered to the ground for a moment, eyes softening before they turned hard again.

"Answer me," I said, pushing my gun harder against her forehead.

"No," she said. "We're acquaintances. I met him in Italy. He helped me out of a rough life."

I felt so shitty. First, she had taken Tommy, and now, she knew Alessandro. And what the hell did she mean that she needed to get information out of him? What kind of information had Tommy had that I didn't?

"Alessandro is in trouble," she said.

Trouble? Alessandro was in trouble? What had happened in Jersey? Did he get—

"He's being tortured at your father's home. We need to save him."

"Why should I trust you?" I asked, narrowing my eyes at her.

Something wasn't right. Why was Dad holding and torturing him? What had happened when he was gone? Was that why he hadn't answered my texts?

"You should trust me because all I want is revenge. I want to kill that man. Ricinni, Sicilian Mafia don. After I do … you can do anything you want to me. I'll let you kill me, torture me for sleeping with your boyfriend. Just let me kill him first." She actually sounded desperate and not in that whorish way. She needed revenge for something. And … by the sound of it, that something was bad.

My hand tightened around the gun, and I wanted nothing more than to put a bullet straight through her head, yet I couldn't get myself to pull the trigger.

"You help me find Alessandro, and I get to do whatever the hell I want to do to you."

She nodded and turned toward the door. "Come on."

36

chiara

"WE'RE GOING to Alessandro's place. He has everything we need." I slid into her car and stared out the windshield, my chest tightening more with every moment that went by.

She started the car and sped down the road, getting onto the highway toward Alessandro's place as if she had been there many times before.

Was I stupid to blindly trust the woman who had slept with my boyfriend? Hell yes.

But if what she had said was true … that Alessandro was in trouble? He might not want a relationship with me now or ever, but I cared about him and wanted him to be safe. In this entire family, he was the only person I could trust. And that was saying something.

"Why'd they take him?" I whispered.

All I could imagine were the cruel things they were probably doing to him. Beating him. Torturing him. Hurting him. All for what? What had he done that was so wrong?

She stayed silent for a long time, then glanced at me. "We were kids," she whispered. "Just kids … and they took some of us from our families. Others were willingly given to the Sicilian Mafia for money and drugs and alcohol." She turned on to the exit. "They did stuff to us and made us do things with other people, grown men and women, in dirty hotel rooms until we were crying. Some got traded away, some were killed, and others stayed and endured it until they couldn't any longer."

All I could hear was pain in her voice. Her hand tightened around the steering wheel, and she shook her head, as if trying to get rid of bad memories.

"Alessandro was one of the first to get out alive, six years old …" Her voice was barely above a whisper. "Seven."

After swallowing hard, she pulled up to the side of the road and parked. "Changed his name, grew up, joined the same mafia that had hurt him, just to get us out. If it wasn't for him, I'd probably be dead."

My heart sank as I heard the horrifying things that had happened to Alessandro *and* her in the past.

The Sicilian Mafia was trafficking children, selling them off and hurting them.

"The Sicilian Mafia started to question him, and he knew that the only way he'd be safe was to prove himself and his importance to the family so they'd keep him, and then he could continue to save children. So, he admitted to drug charges and went to prison for the don. But in prison, he cut a deal to tell the authorities about what was really going on for a lighter sentence."

My hands balled into fists, and I shook my head to try to stay strong.

"And my family? Why does my family have him?" I asked.

She looked over at me and didn't say anything for a long time.

My eyes widened, and I shook my head harder this time. "No. No, I don't believe it. I … you're lying."

"Chiara, I'm sorry."

But I couldn't believe it. The family I had grown up with was in the business of taking children and selling them to the highest bidder, letting them get molested and hurt and raped by anyone who could pay? What the fuck had happened to racketeering and drugs? Had that not been enough for them and they had to resort to taking fucking children?

I punched the dashboard over and over and over until my knuckles bled. Tears streamed down my cheeks. My vision blurred. "No," I cried. "No. They couldn't. They can't do this," I said.

She pulled me to her chest, holding me steady until I stopped freaking out. I grasped on to her arm, knowing that I had no right to cry when she had been through this and experienced this herself.

"Why? Why would they do this to innocent children?"

"Alessandro told me that your family always gives you bullshit to do for them. Why do you think they didn't want you to have any responsibility? Always telling you that you could go on business next time, just never with them?"

I grasped on to her tighter, my chest tightening even more. It all made perfect fucking sense. I saw it now … all of it. Mom always used to hide me in the back room when Dad did business or had business *partners* over. She'd tell me not to make a sound and play with me until they left.

She had known.

Mom knew about this, and she had to have been trying to stop it. She wouldn't let something like this happen.

And they killed her.

They'd fucking killed her for it.

And I would kill them. Every last one of them until this business was mine and *I* could be the one to stop this terror.

37

chiara

WE NEEDED A PLAN. Not a good plan, but a great one. We couldn't walk into Dad's house and demand they let Alessandro go because they wouldn't. We would be gunned down the moment we stepped onto the property, especially once they figured out we had killed all of the men that they'd sent after us.

I paced around the room.

Think, Chiara. Think. What would Dad do in this situation?

Because if I wanted to beat the don, I had to think like him.

"Get out." I tossed her the keys to Alessandro's apartment and slid into the driver's seat. "Find everything you can. Guns. Bullets. Weapons. Anything we can use against them. He has a female friend from Italy who's here. Find her. I'll be back."

She looked into the car, brows furrowed, and shook her head. "Where are you going?"

"I have some business I have to take care of," I said, starting the car. "I'll be back in an hour."

And then I took off down the empty streets toward the police station to find William. He might've been compromised, but I could get him back. I knew I could. All I needed was some information to give him about the mafia, and he'd take them down in the biggest case of the entire decade.

He had been trying to get them for years now. Maybe he had gotten paid off last time, but I knew he wouldn't pass up an opportunity to put the Mafia away. He'd shoot to the top of his department if he did.

I pulled up to the station, checked to see if he was in, then drove to his house when I realized he wasn't. I didn't knock on the door; I barged right into the house, up the stairs, and into his bedroom. I turned the bedroom lights on to blind him and shoved him awake.

"Get up, William. I have information for you."

William blinked his eyes open and sat up in the bed. "Chiara, it's almost four in the morning. What's going on? What do you want?"

"I'll give you whatever you need to take down the mafia," I said, knowing that Alessandro and I had absolutely no way of doing this all by ourselves. If we had cops with us, they could distract some of Dad's guards in the crossfire while I snuck Alessandro out of there.

"What kind of information?" he asked, pulling on a robe.

And so I told him everything, knowing that it might bite me in the ass one day. I swore I would testify. I swore I would get all the evidence that they needed. Pictures, signatures, anything.

William shook his head. "And you expect me to trust you blindly?"

I furrowed my brows at him for a moment, wondering why he wasn't jumping on the offer.

After sighing, he shook his head. "I'll let the station know. My shift doesn't start for another three hours."

"I don't give a fuck when your shift starts. I need this now."

"Chiara, please. It'll take a while anyway to get everyone organized."

I clenched my jaw. "Well, call them now and organize it."

He stared at me for a few moments, then picked up his phone. But as he was about to call his partner, Dad's number popped up on his phone. I pulled the gun out of my waistband, stuck it to his head, and flared my nostrils.

"Hand me the phone," I said through clenched teeth.

He handed me the phone, and I immediately pushed the call to voicemail before looking through his long text messages with Dad, which dated back more than a year. His eyes widened slightly, and he snatched the phone back and tossed it onto the bed, swallowing hard.

"I can explain," he said, shaking. "It's not what it seems like, Chiara, I promise."

"You've been bought this entire time, haven't you?" I asked, staring him right in the eye. When he didn't answer me, I put the gun right to his temple. "How long? Tell me how long you've been aiding those assholes."

William shook his head. I shoved him against the wall, held the gun pointed to his head, and grabbed the rope restraints we used to fuck around with during sex from his dresser. After tying his hands behind his back, I shoved him into a chair, grabbed a knife from the kitchen, and cut his pinky off.

"Every second you waste, I take another one off. Tell me."

Another second. Another finger.

"Now, William."

His middle finger.

He let out a choked scream, but I continued.

"One more time, and you lose the fucking hand."

"The entire time," he finally said.

I wrapped a shirt around his hand to stop the bleeding and shook my head.

"The entire time," he sputtered, face scrunched up in pain, "your father wanted me to act as if I were hunting them down." He winced. "He told me to distract you, to give you something to do to make it seem like you were useful." Another groan left his mouth. "But he threatened to kill everyone and—"

I didn't want to listen to it anymore. I punched him straight in the jaw.

Dad wasn't the man I'd thought he was. He had never been the man I'd thought he was.

He was a villain and a coward.

38

chiara

WE SAT in one of Alessandro's many cars. This one was an inconspicuous black SUV with tinted windows. Parked outside Dad's property, we waited and watched, trying to figure out a way to get into the damn place.

There must've been hundreds of men with guns guarding the property. Most of them I didn't even recognize. They must've been from the Sicilian Mafia—the *best*. These guys weren't average. They looked professional.

The woman who had healed me a few days ago sat in the backseat, saying something in Italian. I stared at her through the rearview mirror and furrowed my brows, only picking up on a couple of words from her. Maybe this was why Dad hadn't taught me Italian, growing up. I'd tried to learn, begged for a tutor, but he'd refused, telling me that it was useless. But I knew better now.

It wasn't useless. Dad was just a dick.

"This won't work," I said, shaking my head.

There were too many people around. One of us was bound to get shot and killed. We needed another way … but how? How were we going to get—

"Fuck." I leaned forward in the passenger seat. "We have to go back to Officer William's house. I have an idea."

Karrie looked over at me. "Are you sure? We don't have much time. They'll figure it out sooner or later that you killed all his men, and your dad will have even more out, tracking you. I'd be surprised if he hasn't already sent them."

"It's the only way," I said, gazing around to make sure nobody had spotted us yet. I knew exactly where Dad had set up his cameras and the places the guards looked, which ones slacked, which ones didn't.

Karrie threw the car in reverse and drove us back onto the highway as I directed her toward Detective William' house. I ran into the house, grabbed his cruiser keys, and handed them to one of Alessandro's partners, who slid into the car.

I leaned through the window. "There are underground tunnels," I said. "My mom took me there one time when Dad had a freaking gunfight with a rival family. I faintly remember where they are, but they'll take us directly toward where Dad must be torturing Alessandro."

It was a long shot, but I had to trust myself. Mom had died for this, and I wouldn't let her death be forgotten. I'd find Alessandro alive, and I'd keep him alive. There was no fucking stopping an angry daughter in red-bottomed shoes who wanted the world to burn.

"You'll distract the guards out front with the police car. Put the lights on when Karrie texts you. Don't get captured. If they start to approach or shoot at the car, leave it there with the lights on and run like hell in the opposite direction."

Stomach tightening, I told myself this was our only hope … because, well, it was. We had one shot at this, and if we didn't succeed, then we'd die in the hands of Dad and the family tonight too.

One shot. One fucking shot.

I grabbed each of their hands and squeezed. I didn't know either of them, I didn't like either of them, but I'd protect both of them.

They were family.
    "Stay safe," I whispered.

39

alessandro

WITH MY HANDS cuffed above my head, I took another punch to the abdomen. It was already bloody and bruised, open wounds and gashes leaking blood. I hung my head and thought of the only things that used to get me through nights and days of abuse when I was younger.

Having a loving mother who wouldn't have sold me out.

Being part of a family that actually loved me.

All fantasies and dreams.

But one day, I wanted them to be real. I wanted that family. I wanted to have kids. I wanted to love and protect them. I wanted them to know that they'd always be safe when they were with me.

And the only person who came to mind when I thought about the future I wanted was Chiara. Sure, she was annoying, always in my way, wanting to do things her way, and sometimes clueless—especially with what went on in her family—but she was so fucking strong and relentless.

Maybe if things were different, we'd be able to be happy together. But things weren't different at all. They were hopeless. Absolutely hopeless.

Another punch to the mouth this time, and I spat up more blood.

Even if she ended up coming here and finishing me off, they'd kill her afterward. She'd be all happy that she was finally part of the family, but then she'd turn around to see her father's gun to her forehead, and she'd die a painful death.

"Listen, you fucking son of a bitch," Chiara's father said to me. "When she gets here, you don't say a fucking word about this business to her. She doesn't find out shit, or she dies too."

I clenched my jaw and spat my blood at him. "You and I both know that she knows too much about your fucking *business* already. You wouldn't let her walk out of here alive. You'd kill her, like you killed your own wife."

He hit me harder against the face, this time with a set of brass knuckles. For a moment, it went dark, and my vision was so cloudy that I couldn't see straight … but I wasn't going to let him off the hook that easily.

"You fucking had her killed," I repeated, unable to even keep my head up. "You're a fucking liar, betrayer. What will Chiara do when she finds out that you killed her mother? She'll hate you, fucking despise you, and—"

There was only rage in his eyes as he hit me again and again and—

His phone rang, and my heart sank. It was probably Tommy, telling this son of a bitch that the job had been completed. That Chiara was dead. It had to be.

He answered it, angry, then slammed the phone down furiously. "She killed them. All of them. Chiara is coming."

40

chiara

THE UNDERGROUND TUNNELS were hot and humid. Beads of sweat dripped down my chest and between my breasts as we walked through them with dim flashlights and as much ammo as we could hold.

Karrie stopped for a moment to catch her breath and wiped some sweat off her forehead with the back of her hand. "Do you know how much longer? I don't know if I'll have cell service down here to tell her to put the police car lights on."

I closed my eyes and tried hard to retrace my steps from so many years ago, but it was difficult because these tunnels seemed to go on forever. It was easy to get lost down here.

I frowned at her. "Maybe ten more—"

"Fuck!" someone yelled, the sound echoing through the dark tunnels.

My eyes widened, and I shut off the flashlight, glancing toward the noise. "Maybe more like a minute," I whispered.

Karrie inched closer to me and pulled out her gun as I began to hear people talking.

"Chiara is fucking coming," Dad said.

Closer. We walked closer, careful not to stumble over anything in the dark.

Glancing beyond the edge of the tunnel, I could see into Dad's personal torture chambers. Chained up by the wrists, Alessandro hung with his head low. It was almost as if he didn't have the strength to hold himself upright. My heart ached for him as I saw the pool of blood beneath his feet.

He didn't deserve this. He'd only wanted to help.

I scanned the room. There were at least twenty men down here alone. I couldn't imagine how many were upstairs, in the house, guarding the perimeter. We were screwed, but this was our only option.

"Twenty," I whispered. "At least."

What the fuck were we going to do? We couldn't go in there with that many men. That was a suicide mission, a death wish—exactly what Dad would want.

I eyed the tunnel across the way. It connected to the tunnel we were in and was even darker than this one. I nodded to it, and we snuck over quietly as I instructed Karrie to make the call.

"All right," I whispered. "We lure them out, run to the end of this tunnel, and kill them when they turn the corners. They'll come five at a time. We kill as many as we can that way, and then we go in there."

Karrie nodded, and I aimed my gun to the ground and shot a bullet into the dirt. As soon as the gun went off, Karrie and I made a run for it. As expected, five of Dad's guards jogged into the tunnel with their guns pointed at the end of it.

They walked so slowly toward the end, and when they were in range, we killed all five of them within a few seconds. The tunnels went silent again.

"Did you kill them?" Dad said to someone.

I'd kill to see if he was shitting himself right now.

When nobody answered, we heard more footsteps. Five men appeared, slowly walking down toward us, and received the same fate as the others. I grabbed their guns and threw them aside, so even if one was alive still, they wouldn't be able to kill us.

"Is the job done?" Dad asked again to someone who must've been in the family.

This time, his voice was a tad bit fearful.

One pair of footsteps this time, and Dad appeared. He took his gun and shot ahead into the darkness, not caring who the fuck he hit. My heart raced fast, and all I wanted to do was shoot back at him, so that was what I did.

Aiming my gun around the corner, I shot a bullet, hoping it hit his foot. He cursed out loud when something made contact, and I knew it was now or never. So, I nodded to Karrie, and we ran as quickly as we could. Ready to die to save Alessandro and eliminate this madness.

Like the coward he was, Dad sprinted into the chambers, yelling something in Italian. From above, I heard the muffled sound of police sirens, and Dad yelled again about people going back upstairs to see what it was all about.

With guns blazing, people blindly fired bullets around the room as they ran in all directions. When we entered the chambers, it was pure chaos. Absolute chaos. I knew exactly where Alessandro was and I shot out the lights and ran over to him to unchain him.

"Chiara," he whispered, eyes barely open enough to see me. "Chiara, you shouldn't be here."

"Shut the fuck up," I said, thrusting a gun into his hand and hurrying to kill some more guards.

All I wanted to do was find Dad and kill that asshole for hurting me and Mom and all those kids.

But Dad was gone. I couldn't find him anywhere. Not a dead body. Not with a guard with a gun. Nowhere. I sprinted up the stairs and through the house to find it completely empty. From the window, I watched a car peel out of the driveway and race down the road.

Sprinting back down the stairs, I tried to find a set of keys, but couldn't find any. So, I let him go. As much as it fucking hurt me, I let the bastard go so I could help Alessandro and the others get out of this mess safely.

I ran back down into the cells to find Alessandro and the Sicilian Mafia boss. Alessandro held him by the collar and was raining punch after punch down on his face. My eyes widened slightly as I watched every muscle in his back flex as he beat the shit out of the guy until he was unconscious. And even then, he continued to hit him until the guy didn't move.

All the other guards were dead, and we were one step closer to ending Dad's reign.

41

chiara

I STARED out the police car window, watching the rain fall outside of it. Alessandro sat in the backseat with Karrie, talking about how the Sicilian Mafia would either dissolve quickly or be taken over by a rival family. His fight was over, but mine was far from it.

Dad was still out there, and I had to find him before he found me. I didn't know how I was going to do it without my *family* after me. They knew I was going to go to Alessandro's place. They knew I was with Alessandro and his posse. They knew that I was full of rage and wouldn't stop until they all died.

My eyes became teary for some reason, but I blinked the tears away. This wasn't a time to cry. I had no right. I hadn't been through hell and back, like Alessandro had. I was just some spoiled brat Mafia boss's daughter who hadn't known shit until about twelve hours ago.

"Finally," Alessandro said to Karrie. "Finally fucking killed the bastard."

I glanced at him through the rearview mirror to see the relief on his face. He looked over at me, and our eyes met for a brief moment. He was bruised and beaten badly from the torture, his eyes black and bloody. I mustered up my best half-smile, to which he responded with a frown.

After glancing away, I pulled into Alessandro's apartment building lot. We walked to the elevators, waited in the stuffy room to get to the top, and made it into his apartment.

Escaping and stopping someone like that must've been hard for him to do. It'd taken years, but Alessandro hadn't stopped until he got all his revenge. I was a proud friend to him and even these two girls. I didn't know either of them, but they'd fought hard for something they believed in.

"What's wrong?" Karrie asked as Alessandro patched himself up.

I was happy for Alessandro, but I was sad for our relationship… if I could even call this little thing that.

Now that he had gotten his revenge, I didn't know if he'd go back to Italy or not. Would we even talk anymore? After all the shit we'd been through, he probably wanted me out of his hair and to relax while he had the time.

"I should go," I whispered, not knowing why I was saying this at all.

But something inside of me told me that I should leave. Alessandro and the girls should celebrate this achievement, and I had absolutely no place here, especially if he didn't want anything to do with me.

Besides, how could I stay around someone who I wanted to love … when he didn't want the same thing? Was I supposed to act as if I didn't love the fuck out of him? Like we were just coworkers in a really, really bad job?

"No," Alessandro said, narrowing his eyes at me. But he still didn't move or smile or make any slight adjustments to his behavior to make it seem like he wanted me here. "Stay."

42

chiara

ALESSANDRO GLANCED OVER AT ME, and I looked away from him and walked to the window to stare down at the city, feeling quite … vulnerable. Dad was still out there with a handful of his guards who were stupid enough to protect him with their lives. But that wasn't why I felt so unguarded. It was because Alessandro knew exactly how I felt about him, he knew why I'd saved him, and he probably even knew that I loved him.

Dad had always told me to be guarded, to never trust anyone … but that was all I seemed to want to do when I was with Alessandro. I wanted him to capture me with his tongue, whisper all those sweet nothings in my ear, tell me that he loved me, too, even if he didn't really mean it.

"Leave," Alessandro said to Karrie and his medic, washing some blood from his hands.

I heard quick footsteps, and then the front door shut. My eyes fluttered closed quickly, and I sucked in a deep breath, breathing in his scent. He stood directly behind me, wrapped his hand around the front of my throat, and pulled me closer to him.

"What you did was dangerous," he said into my ear with such anger and annoyance in his voice.

Rage built inside of me as I turned on my heel and shoved him away from me. But he caught my wrist before I could do anything.

"Screw you, Alessandro. If I hadn't saved you, you'd be dead."

"Karrie told me you were worried about me," he said, a smirk crawling onto his face.

I tried to shove him back again. But he pushed me against the window, his lips brushing against my ear.

My breath caught in the back of my throat. "Fuck you, Alessandro," I whispered, unable to get anything out but that. I balled my hands into fists yet relaxed as his lips pressed against the crook of my neck. "A fucking *thank you* would be nice," I said through clenched teeth. Yet a *thank you* wasn't what I wanted.

He picked me up off the ground–albeit with a bit of a stumble from his injuries–and my legs instinctively wrapped around his torso. "You looked fucking sexy with that gun in your hand," he said, nibbling on my earlobe. "I'm hard, just thinking about it."

He rocked his hips into mine, and I sucked in a deep breath, feeling his hardness press against my core.

Fuck, I wanted it so bad.

I wanted *him* so bad.

"You're welcome," I said sarcastically.

"I want you," he said suddenly. "Forget what I said the other day about not wanting to be with you, Chiara. I want you." He walked toward his bedroom with me, his hands gripping my ass, his mouth all over my neck. "And I'm going to have you."

Resting one hand behind my head, he laid me back on the bed, pressing needy kisses down my neck. I ran my hands over his body, tugging his shirt over his head and kicking off his pants, being careful not to hurt him. He must've been so sore from earlier.

He crawled between my parted legs and held them apart, dipping his head to my stomach and kissing below my navel. Lying between my legs, he pulled down my pants, interlocked his fingers with mine, and started to eat me out.

My back arched, and I grasped his fingers tighter. Pleasure pulsed through my body, my legs slowly starting to tremble. I moaned out and felt his face drop even lower to my entrance, his tongue working its magic.

I stared down at Alessandro, my stomach in knots and a strong wave of emotion threatening to come over me. Alessandro wanted me. He really wanted me.

I curled my hand into his hair. "Alessandro, please …"

"Please what?" he asked, glancing up at me, face still buried between my legs.

"Take me," I whispered.

He kissed back up my body, sucking on my nipple and grasping my tits softly. I clenched when the head of his cock brushed against my aching pussy. He pressed his lips to mine in one lingering kiss, then rested his forehead against mine and pushed himself inside of me slowly.

I dug my fingers into his shoulders, moaning against his lips. He brushed his thumb against my cheekbone and stared down into my eyes so passionately and intimately. I wrapped my arms around his neck and pulled him toward me. As soon as our lips collided, he started to pump in and out more quickly. His tongue slipped into my mouth. His lips devoured mine.

When he broke our kiss, he tugged me to his chest. I dug my fingers into his muscles, feeling his heart racing under them.

"Chiara," he whispered into my ear, snaking an arm under my neck, "I love you."

My heart almost stopped when he said those words, my pussy clenching around him. Alessandro loved me? The words sounded so small inside my head, yet felt so earth-shattering. I dug my fingers into him and bucked my hips against his.

He pounded deeper inside of me, and my walls clenched around him. The pressure built higher and higher and higher in my core.

"Oh God, Alessandro," I moaned, arching my back. "I love you too."

He stuffed his face back into the crook of my neck, pressed his lips below my ear, and sucked on my skin. His body tensed, and I could feel his cock pulsing inside of me, filling me with his cum. I cried out, my body trembling against his, my walls pulsing around his cock.

My body tingled in delight, wave after wave of pleasure rushing through me. Everything was so much more intense than the last time we'd had sex, all my emotions raw. He pulled out of me slowly and lay on the bed next to me.

He rested his forehead against mine. "I love you so fucking much. You're all I could think about. I thought I'd never see you again. But you're mine now, and you'll be mine forever."

43

chiara

SITTING in Alessandro's car after making up with him, I swayed my feet back and forth underneath the dashboard and watched him pull out into the dark, dreary New York street at five-thirty a.m. He pulled to the corner of Albany and South End Avenue and cut the lights. He leaned back in his seat and sighed quietly, fixing his gaze on the foggy edges of the windshield. Rain hammered against the Benz.

A single streetlight flickered above us, illuminating the letters C.A.C. etched into the grip of the 9mm that sat in my lap.

"You know what you have to do," Alessandro said after a few moments, tapping his fingers against the steering wheel.

We needed to find a place to stay, but he had his focus on killing Dad as soon as possible.

"A bullet through his head will make us a target for the rest of the family," I said.

But I already knew we were a target for the rest of the family. They were in hot shit and had to get rid of me as quickly as possible, before word got out about who they were and what they did to innocent kids.

Red and blue lights flashed in my rearview mirror as a police car pulled up behind us.

Alessandro swore under his breath, "Shit."

Two figures exited the car. One of them stepped into a puddle near the curb.

I traced my initials on my gun with the tip of my finger, then wrapped my hand around the rubber grip. Alessandro pulled a single bronze bullet from his pocket and handed it to me. The bullet brought back memories of this past week. The haunting image of a car rolling into the river, the stench of gunpowder and blood seeping into the seats of my car, the bullets ricocheting off of my car.

One bullet, one death sentence.

Alessandro shifted in his seat and stared at me with those gray, dangerous eyes. "Do you think your father deserves to live?"

"Does anyone who has done what he has deserve to live?"

I hid my gun in my waistband and stuffed the bullet into my pocket. The only life that mattered in this business was your own.

An officer tapped three times on my window and shone a flashlight into the car.

"What're you doing out here?" he asked.

"Just enjoying the weather," Alessandro said to him, smiling at the man.

The officer looked further into the car at me, furrowed his brows, and frowned. "Do I know you?" he asked, giving me a weird look.

"No," I said, suppressing an eye roll and smiling sweetly at him.

He must've been new.

I leaned forward and watched as his eyes dropped to my tits. "Do I know *you*?"

Eyes flickering to mine once more, he grimaced and looked back at Alessandro. "You shouldn't be out this late. Go back home. A storm is coming."

Then, without asking another question, the cops disappeared back into their car and waited for us to move.

"Hotel?" Alessandro asked.

"No ..." My lips curled into a small smile. "Officer William's home."

44

chiara

OFFICER WILLIAM SAT, tied up in his home with a gag in his mouth and tears staining his cheeks. I didn't give a single fuck about him, but I could tell that Alessandro wanted to kill his ass for ever sleeping with me. Alessandro paced the room with his gun in his hand.

I placed William's cell phone on the table in front of him. "You're going to call my dad," I said to him, crouching by his side.

He stared at me with teary eyes and shook his head.

I grasped his chin and forced him to nod. "If you want to live, you're going to call him and tell him to meet you here. Tell him you have me in your custody. Tell him that I'm being charged with murdering his guards. Don't—*do not*—fuck it up. You do whatever you have to do to get him to come here."

Alessandro grabbed a fistful of his hair and pulled it back so William stared directly up at him. "If you seem nervous or if he figures out that you're lying, I'll kill you and your entire family. Do you understand?"

After he nodded, Alessandro ripped the duct tape from his mouth.

William let out a whimper and looked at me. "Chiara, please, let me go. This isn't you. Please, don't—"

I picked up his phone and dialed Dad's number, which he had on speed dial.

Almost immediately, William shut his mouth. The phone rang a few times.

"Make this quick," Dad said through the phone.

"I have Chiara," William said, glancing at me. He parted his lips and pressed them back together, as if he wanted to say something but thought better of it. "Just wanted to see what you want me to do with her before I… I, uhm, take her down to the station."

"Bitch," Dad said over the phone.

All I wanted to do was wrap my hands around his throat and kill that bastard. It wasn't a choice anymore. I had to do it, not for myself or for Mom, but for everyone.

Dad paused. "Ricardo's. Ten minutes. Don't be late."

"You'll have to hurry," William said. "I don't have much time before my boss finds out."

Dad grumbled, and then the line went dead. He didn't have to answer for me to know that he was coming. He was desperate to end this madness once and for all. He wanted to kill me so I couldn't snitch on him.

I shut the phone off and tossed it aside, glancing at Alessandro. "Prepare."

45

chiara

WHEN DAD PULLED into the driveway, I hid in the other room and picked up the 9mm with my initials on the grip. I had used it several times before, but never to execute someone like this.

When Dad knocked on the door, Alessandro answered with his gun pointed right at his head and pulled him into the house. Alessandro shoved him into the room and onto the handcrafted wooden chair next to William. He bound Dad's hands behind his back with thick silver wire and covered his mouth with a piece of duct tape, tying him to the chair.

For years, I had waited to kill the man who put a hit on my mother's head, and today, I finally would. I didn't care if it made me a target or not. I turned to face Dad for the first time since this morning.

My father gazed up at me with wide brown eyes. Brown eyes that I used to trust.

For fifteen minutes, I stared him down, telling myself I could do this.

Alessandro ripped off the tape. Dad tried fumbling around to stand, but Alessandro pushed him back down.

Not all high and mighty now.

"Whatever this *pezzo di merda* has told you is a lie, *tesoro*. You would be a fool to believe anything. He's betrayed the Sicilian Mafi—"

"You had Mom killed."

My cheeks flushed in anger, and then he gave me the look I had always hated. Every emotion drained from his face, and his lips curled into a snarl. This was not my father. This was the man who had paid a man to have his wife shot and killed in the street.

"What're you going to do, Chiara? Shoot me?"

I raised the gun to my father's head, my fingers trembling. This was the end of his reign. It had to be.

Alessandro stepped closer to me, placing his lips near my ear. "Put a bullet through his head, *reginetta*, or I will."

I pressed the muzzle against his forehead, and my father finally recognized the woman he had raised. Strong, independent, deadly.

He shook his head. "*Tesoro*, please. I'll let you run the business if that's what you want, give you more responsibility, anything."

Even now, he was telling me what he thought I wanted to hear. What a shitty father he was.

Nobody, except Alessandro, believed in me until I was threatening their life. Not Tommy. Not even my own father. I'd had enough of the lies and the betrayal that seemed to plague this family.

The first gunshot rang through the air. Then the next. Then the next. One after another, in quick succession, until all the bullets had pierced my father's skull.

His body smacked against the ground, and a puddle of thick red blood pooled beneath him.

It was over the second he'd ordered the hit.

I stared down at his body. "The damage could not be undone," I said.

46

chiara

PEOPLE from the family gathered in Il Giardino del Cancio with cigars, guns, and bottles of sambuca. There were so many people that they spilled out onto the sidewalks. I guess word traveled quickly about my father. From the outside, all I could hear was arguing about who was going to be the next don of the mafia and leader of this family.

It was a bunch of men who thought they were better than everyone else, who thought they could lead better than anyone else, who thought they deserved being the boss more than anyone else.

But there was only one person who deserved this.

Me.

I pushed through the family men and walked right into the restaurant, getting dirty looks and being called a whore. With my gun in one hand and Alessandro's hand in the other, I refused to listen to them. I was ready to kill anyone who wanted to test me today.

Instead, I walked right up to the bar and stood on top of the counter. "Shut the fuck up!"

They ignored me and continued shouting and arguing with each other.

Having had enough, I cocked my gun and shot a bullet right through the counter underneath me to get their attention. Everyone went silent again, one hand on their gun, and looked up at me.

Some yelled that I was a traitor. Others told me to get my whore ass off the counter. Alessandro responded to one of them with a punch right in the throat. I watched the man drop his gun and fall to the ground, gasping for breath.

I cleared my throat. "None of you will be the next leader of this family," I said.

Some of the men started chuckling, and I silenced them with another bullet into the counter.

"I am the next leader of this family, and if any of you want to challenge me for the spot, then step up," I said with so much anger in my voice, daring them to do something.

More men started chuckling.

"I'm serious," I said. "None of you knows how to run a business anyway. You're clueless and useless."

"So, what, we're going to let a woman run the family?" someone yelled out, which earned him a cheer of laughter.

I tightened my grip on my gun and squeezed hard. "Yes."

He stood up from the back and shook his head. "No. I'm not going to let—"

I shot him straight through the head. Blood splattered everywhere, and he stumbled back, hit the wall, and slid down it. Dead.

I stared around at everyone else. "Who else? Which one of you *stronzos* wants to die next?"

Another man stood up by the windows, and I put a bullet in his head, not blinking once.

The men started to whisper, yet none of them stood up to challenge me.

I looked around. "Who else?" I asked. "Do it now because if you try to challenge me later, you won't get an easy death. I'll hang your family by their fucking toes and make you watch as they bleed out to death."

Everyone stopped, eyes widening. After a few moments, when nobody else said a word, I dusted off my shirt.

"Good, because I'm about to clean this family up. I'm running this place differently. Nobody touches a fucking child. Nobody *thinks* about touching a child. If I hear word that you are going against that one and only demand of mine—even if it's a fucking rumor—you're dead."

I wouldn't allow that child-trafficking shit. We were professionals, and it was about damn time they started acting like it.

The End

also by emilia rose

Paranormal Romance

Submitting to the Alpha

Come Here, Kitten

My Werewolf Professor

The Twins

Four Masked Wolves

Monster Lover

Contemporary Romance

Stepbrother

Poison

The Bad Boy

Detention

Excite Me

Mafia Boss

Mafia Toy

about the author

Emilia Rose is a USA Today bestselling author of steamy romance. She loves writing about dirty-talking bad boys who are obsessed with innocent, and sometimes insecure, virgin heroines. She currently lives in a small town in Connecticut USA with her husband and three playful cats.

Join Emilia's newsletter for exclusive giveaways, early chapter releases, and more!

also by emilia rose

Scan the QR code with your phone to view all of Emilia's books!

www.ingramcontent.com/pod-product-compliance
Lightning Source LLC
Chambersburg PA
CBHW020821190726
48285CB00006B/2372